EXULTATION
Erotic Tales of Divine Union

by

Jacqueline Sa

Published by

Roots
& Legends®

www.rootslegends.com

Soft cover and E-book first published January 2012
Second edition first published March 2013
Third edition first published March 2014
by Roots & Legends®
www.rootslegends.com
ISBN: 978-0-9840324-0-2 (sc)
ISBN: 978-0-9840324-1-9 (e)

Library of Congress Control Number: 2011940764

Printed in the United States of America

Original cover art © Gaelyn Larrick (www.gaelynlarrick.com)
Original illustrations © Tory Elena (www.toryelena.com)
Poem: *Rendezvous* © Anitah L. Gambos (www.moontideproductions.com)
Poem: *Earth's Revelations* © Jacqueline Sa
Book design by Christer Rowan (www.rowandesign.com)

Further praise for

EXULTATION
Erotic Tales of Divine Union

"FOR EVERYONE whose heart resonates with the multitude of levels of entities in this creation, these novels place the sexual experiences of us humans in a force field of attraction that breaks the confines of our every day normality."
—CARL JOHAN CALLEMAN, Author of *The Mayan Calendar and the Transformation of Consciousness* and *The Purposeful Universe*

"WITHIN EVERY sacredly portrayed story of Jacqueline Sa's book, one feels guided through the ethers of Great Mystery. Important knowledge and wisdom are shared—unique ancient messages that serve as guidance to life in these fast-evolving times are revealed... One senses the integration of one's heart with the other dimensions of spiritual union... One feels absorbed and enriched with an inner understanding of life's new consciousness that is emanating from the ancient roots of the universe's Tree of Life."
—SEAN CAULFIELD, Artist of sacred rock art, Africa

"JACQUELINE TAKES US into the heart of our own desire and opens us there. She transmutes flesh to spirit, spirit to flesh and turns you on in the telling of the tale."
—ROSS KERSEY, Expanded Sexual Awareness Course Leader

"FOR MILLENNIA, yogis practice the art of union, unifying all elements. Jacqueline brings this age-old concept, which the West has not embraced to the forefront. Awakening our deep desire to be whole, by uniting the male and female unconditionally, we find our true selves in each other."
—IRENE KAI, Author of Golden Mountain

"EXULTATION—the very word as defined in the dictionary means the art or condition of rejoicing greatly. Many of us need to 'rejoice greatly' that Jacqueline has fulfilled her pledge to write about ending the divisions of the sexes, and that our longing for union that our hearts have carried for eons can now be realized. This book is immensely rich with layered textures of knowledge and wisdom that could only be brought forth at this time."
—KAREN SCHNEIDER, MA, DCH, Teacher, Healer, Minister

"THE SEVEN divine erotic tales in Exultation are the new Seven Wonders of the World, heralding the new Heaven and Earth. Sting sings "love is the 7th wave," and this book is the leading edge crest of that wave, accelerating us into a revolutionary era of union and creation. Don't be left behind in the stagnant old order. Surf this tsunami of healing, radical love with Jacqueline into impossible beauty and rapture."
—BOB SHINE, Uni-verse poet and artist

Dedicated to

Our Life-Giving Lady Earth
Our Progenitor the Sun

All the Lovers who aspire
to co-create Divine Partnership on Earth

Acknowledgments

SENTIENT GUIDANCE from Lady Earth led to the birth of this book. My journey into writing this novel started in China, when I heeded the heartsongs of Earth and thought I would express her stories with a graphic novel. Hu Han Bing, my dear artist friend in Suzhou, had unconditionally given of her love and time to create a number of drawings for me. Her generosity of spirit kept me inspired to pursue the project. Through twists and turns, the book has become this current creation of sensual tales and I regrettably have not been able to use Han Bing's art, but I want to herewith express my gratitude to her.

I am thankful to my book cover artist, Gaelyn Larrick, who has given me relevant pointers in many ways from the beginning, beyond her exquisite design of the book cover.

My deep appreciation goes to Laura Hurst, the original illustration artist of my book's first and second edition (published in 2012 and 2013), who had unreservedly honored Earth, and contributed her original art of many dedicated hours. This current edition has taken a new direction with visionary art by Tory Elena, who rendered multi-dimensional illustrations for the tales, and to whom I give thanks for our collaborative co-visioning.

My respect goes to Anitah Gambos—a soul-reader poet who wrote the poem used in *Love of a Pharaoh*; and Bob Shine—a Sun warrior who indefatigably shared with me his wisdom about the magic of Sun and Earth. I give thanks to Shari Kalb and Anitah for the editing of the stories. A grateful thanks to Christer Rowan, my graphic designer, who meticulously constructed the layout for this book with valuable suggestions.

A SPECIAL TRIBUTE to three amazing men whose contributions go beyond the tangible. To David the Earth shaman who ignited the breath of Lady Earth into my being; to Jeffrey, my kindred soul bond who came in astral form animating me to write the initial stories, and who encouraged me to publish them; to Wei-Li, my soulmate of lifetimes who believed in this book and who motivated me to complete it. My gratitude, love and respect for each of them are beyond words.

EXULTATION
Erotic Tales of Divine Union

Table of Contents

Illustrations

By Tory Elena

* See *About the Artists,* pages 200–201

To My Readers

SINCE MY FIRST PUBLISHING of this book in 2012, many readers had reflected that these stories reverberated certain memories of some inner knowing, familiar yet elusive. Maybe you might resonate with the following insights. My first inkling on writing this book was birthed on a journey to Egypt in 2007, when I was astounded by a 'rendezvous' with a forgotten aspect of my soul who had made a promise to deliver a message—something about healing the chasm between the sexes. I was to write a book on Unity Consciousness and Divine Partnership with 'archetypes from the future', honoring sacred sexuality as homage to the matrix of our galactic wonders—the spark of Singularity of the Original Light in our human hearts.

Then unexpectedly, in the Summer Solstice of 2008, came powerful transmissions from the Spirit of Earth herself, with the potency of her sentience so palpable—expressed with stunning emotions and exhilarated pulsations! Earth's sensibility conveys that she is moving into a higher octave of her own evolution, leading humanity toward an awakening of Eros—for a sublime meaning that goes beyond self-centered gratifications, to embrace an eco-oriented sexuality that expands into

Deep Ecology and cosmos-centered explorations.

Earth is "transmuting from tired, abused and undeserving into fully remembering her devotion to the magnificence in the making!" She no longer wants humanity to rely on her as Mother Earth, but to restore her as Lady Earth with a new respect, for her rightful place in the cosmos.

She appealed to us to honor our own erotic desires as a stirring back to the original burst of cosmic becoming—a euphoric Yes to the sexual creation impulse of the Universe. Channeling this flow into currents of a dervish dance in ecstasy, we become the sacred conduits of releasing the divine energies from within. When we kindle this primordial frequency permeating through every fiber of our being, we render sacred our act of communion. It is this same primal instinct of rapturous intelligence that originates our galactic creative unleashing.

Earth's sentience proliferated a stream of consciousness through me. Interlaced with real-life occurrences, her words gentle yet clear, she guided me through the weaving of the parables—whether in the form of a mermaid singing the ocean alive, of an ancient temple dancer devoted to the Great Goddess, or of Earth-Spirit in sexual bliss with a shaman. Each archetypal embodiment is an emanation of her multi-dimensional facets, metamorphosed into living-beings, from Source itself.

Though the stories in this book are independent of each other, they are interwoven threads that celebrate both the masculine and the feminine offerings of love. Men are acknowledged for their natural thriving through physical love that leads to the opening heart, which inspires their creativity, chivalry and the protection of their beloveds. Women are esteemed in how we love from the core of our very being that is entwined with our sexual passion, receptivity, surrender and kindness. Both expressions of love, in their enlightened states, naturally lead to a compassionate awakening for humanity and for all of life.

As the body is the temple of our soul, what is more sublime than to revel our physical pleasures as a form of attaining enlightenment? When corporal bliss is exulted with reverence as a sacred expression, we co-manifest an ecstatic state to lead one another home, to the essence of cosmic enfolding—the endless bursts of all of creations. No amount of sexual heights can satiate our infinite mind and bottomless soul until we reunite with the erotic impulse of Source itself. This is the alchemy of the "light codes", told in the tale of *Love of a Pharaoh*. Divine sexuality is a cosmocentric intelligence that discharges our own light; it thereby ushers Lady Earth—our World Soul—back into her full glory of never-ending evolution. Our sexual act becomes a consecrated offering to Earth and Sun—our progenitors of life itself—as a ceremony, a purification of purpose beyond biological urges. Celestial eroticism is Exultation in quantum rhapsodies enwrapped in the unified field of Oneness with All There Is.

MAY THESE TALES awaken in you an inspiration to merging body, mind and soul in one delightful union, and sprinkle some delicious spices to your dreams. May the personal be transcended and the Divine be revealed in effervescent ecstasies.

—Jacqueline Sa, February 2014

For further reading, please visit my website: www.RootsLegends.com; and I invite your reflections: unveil@RootsLegends.com.

The Venus Encounter

"I have come to renew your spirit
and re-ignite your passion…
and Venice needs you."

The Venus Encounter

ETHAN was completely frustrated after three intense days of negotiating with the bureaucracy of the Italian Port Authority. His mind was frayed after rounds of heated debates through hand-speaking and excitable translators, about the biggest canal-dredging scheme Venice planned to undertake. This romantic city was about to be transformed into the twenty-first century hub for maritime trade in Europe. Ethan was the key strategist of a global environmental organization that was doing everything it could to alter the course of this insane exploit, which would have dire ecological consequences for this whole region.

A majestic sun was setting amidst the hideous dredging machines that bobbed like large mechanical birds on the calm golden water. Ethan was disheartened with the unending greed and folly of big corporations in collusion with government agencies. He felt so tired from having built his entire career upon fighting the powers that be. Sometimes he wondered what impact his actions really had in the big picture of the deteriorating ecosystem of this fragile planet. He felt his efforts were in vain time and again, no matter how passionately he fought for sustainability or how fervently he tried to stop abusive projects to the land.

To take his mind off such heavy topics, Ethan aimlessly wandered around the Piazza San Marco, looking idly at the flashy merchandise in shameless display. From the corner of his eyes, he caught a glimpse of a stunningly beautiful woman wearing a translucent aqua-blue dress who appeared to float by. Her strides effortlessly revealed the ease and confidence of a local. Her hair was silky black with highlights of gold and her angular profile evoked an ancient exotic allure, but with a definite Italian flair. There were beautiful women from many cultures amidst the hordes of photo-snapping Japanese sightseers on day-tours. Ethan was puzzled why this woman would stand out so much to him. Maybe it was her ethereal quality that took his breath away. She didn't seem to be from this world, yet she had a commanding presence, which distinguished her from the throng of tourists whirling about. The glance she cast his way was surprisingly open and inviting, without the pretense of seduction. He was immediately enthralled; he had never met a woman with an aura of such feminine mastery. His dreamy nature took over and he started fantasizing.

Suddenly, the loud shrill of an island-wide siren

pierced the air and snapped Ethan out of his mesmerized state. Shopkeepers, as though in accustomed reflexes, swiftly pulled merchandise from the floors and started to close up their shops. Ethan asked a shop girl what was happening; she nonchalantly replied with a singsong Italian accent: "*Allora*, it's the flood warning again, but it's not serious. It hasn't flooded in ten years!" The phone rang. She became agitated and barked into the phone while rolling her eyes and gesturing wildly. She hung up, saying, "Oh, it's my mother, she always worries, as though all my merchandise will drown!" Ethan thanked her and sauntered off, giving her space to deal with her armloads of porcelain dolls and carnival figurines on the floor. Everyone was moving fast around him, hurrying somewhere as though to escape an impending flood. He looked for the Beauty in blue but she was nowhere in sight. He was disappointed that the siren had sidetracked him. He dodged into a side street restaurant that was a bit above street level, just in case the flood actually came. He ordered a drink and some food, and made further inquiries. The manager of the restaurant was named Luigino, a jolly gentleman who reassured Ethan that there was nothing to worry about, that he should relax and enjoy himself.

Ethan was finally able to unwind as he savored the steamy plate of linguine, swirling in black squid ink, a specialty of Venice he had come to appreciate. It was only seven in the evening; he had plenty of time before he needed to get on the 8:30 ferry to Lido Island. He was wondering where the Beauty in blue had gone, whether she had panicked and rushed home. He wished he had followed her and offered to chivalrously protect her. Her countenance had left an indelible impression in his heart. He drifted into a make-believe conversation with her about his project in Venice and his life-long passion for environmental issues. He even felt her appreciative understanding and encouragement from the kind expression in her eyes. Every man yearns for supportive acceptance from a woman he adores. She lifted her crystal goblet—filled with an aquamarine elixir that bubbled over the brim—and conveyed to him her admiration. His weariness was magically lifted and his anxiety melted away.

He must have been lost in his reverie and visions of imagining her lovely presence, when Ethan saw Luigino walk in wearing wet, thigh-high boots. He casually and jovially announced that all of Venice was under water. Startled, Ethan rushed to a nearby window and watched in disbelief as the water rose from the canals, inundating all the streets. He apprehensively asked whether he could still catch the ferry. Luigino told him to relax; no ferry would be operating until the water subsided.

Time went by. Luigino offered rounds of complimentary drinks, swiftly snapping his fingers, commanding his waiters to reassure the crowds. The customers didn't look too concerned; everyone seemed to be in a celebratory holiday mood. A little later, Ethan went to check on the water level, which now had risen so high that the people remaining on the streets were all sloshing through with difficulty, knee deep in water. He had been to Venice a few times in the past and he had never seen such an astounding spectacle. The city had fallen into the silence of a ghost town. All the shops were closed and their dazzling lights reflected twisted neon shapes in the glistening darkness. By nine o'clock in the evening Ethan was a bit tipsy and was concerned how he would get back to his hotel in Lido; he really needed a good night's sleep before tomorrow's intense round of meetings. He discussed it with Luigino who amicably suggested that he go back to San Marco square and wait for the ferry announcement.

Luigino gave him two large garbage bags to put on each of his legs as makeshift boots. What a humbling experience this was—waddling like an awkward duck, splattering through the meandering streets and bridges. He was certainly not the elegant sight he so often prided himself to be. As he struggled to find his direction back to the square, he faintly saw a glowing, translucent, aqua-blue apparition floating about fifty feet in front of him like a liquid guiding light leading him out of darkness. He was soaking wet, heart pounding, hoping that this feminine silhouette was the same Beauty he had glimpsed earlier that evening, but feeling insecure about meeting her face-to-face in his less than suave apparel and wet-dog condition.

When he somehow stumbled into the square, she seemed to have disappeared into thin air! With heightened anticipation of finding her again, he almost didn't notice the surreal piazza swaying dreamily on glistening cobblestones. The water had subsided quite a bit, and the night cafés nonchalantly re-opened. Waiters in their white shirts, bow ties, and rolled-up black pants, swiftly set up chairs and tables in the water for the late night concerts. Café au lait and macchiato wafted through the festive air. It is amazing how devoted the

Venetians are to the unending celebration of life, as though the flood were just another heightened prop. The whole square came alive with laughter, smoke, and melodious waltz tunes from the various competing concerts on raised platforms. People danced and clowned around in rolled-up skirts and pants on the lustrous cobblestones. Ethan's mood lightened. Swept up in the romance of this ethereal ambiance, he got rid of his silly garbage bags, rolled up his soaked pants, and cast his ruined shoes to the side. He started twirling with abandon, infected with the joy of being.

Before he blinked open his eyes, the stunning Beauty in blue materialized in his waltzing arms, appearing out of nowhere. He caught a startled breath, but she calmly, lovingly, and serenely looked into his eyes with an exquisite smile. Her waist elegantly swayed under the grip of his fingers. Her semi-wet chiffon dress pressed against her slender body, revealing her sensual silhouette, with a bit of décolleté revealing the pulse of her breasts. Ethan's grip tightened, he wasn't going to let her go this time. She was barefoot and devoid of jewelry. Her black hair glistened intensely in the dark night, her golden wisps even more golden as she whirled with delight. Ethan swore he had never beheld such a splendor and he fell instantly in love—well, lust and desire might be a more accurate description. He achingly wanted her, now!

As though on cue with his bulging urgency, she gracefully and swiftly danced him to a dimly lit corner of a rather deserted side street. With her back against the wall of an old building, she pulled him tightly against her body, raised her face to his, and offered him her slightly parted luscious mouth. He overtook her, avidly probing her sweet taste, licking and nibbling on her lightly, and running his tongue on the inside of her upper lip. At the same time, he was tearing eagerly through her clothes to feel her gorgeous breasts, with nipples so enticingly erect and juicy that it drove him wild with primal lustfulness. He grabbed her bottom with his forceful hands and raised her off the ground so he could relish on her silky bosom. He was lost in the delirium of savoring her heavenly scent, biting and flicking his tongue between her two nipples, which seemed to compete for his full attention. She moaned with intoxicated delight. She ran her hand through his hair, pulling hard and stimulating the erogenous zones of his scalp, which drove him crazy with desire. She deftly loosened his wet shirt and pants and fluttered her fingers on his chest in a tantalizing way that sent a penetrating pleasure through him, making him want more. Her feverish responses matched his intense passion perfectly.

She seemed to have turned into a thousand-armed goddess who could caress every part of him simultaneously. One of her hands fondled his engorged manhood, alternating between firm strokes and a teasingly light touch around the tip, making him feel like he would explode at any moment. She drove him wilder than a wild beast, her hands on his back, caressing and scratching hard all at once. Ethan also felt one of her hands caressing the sensitive inside flesh of his thighs. He was drowning in a trance-like intoxication, releasing all the tension he had held for days in his body. He didn't care if anyone heard their carnal groans. He lifted her dress, exposing a delicate lacy thong. He savagely tore it aside and plunged hard and deep into her inviting black mound. He ravaged her uncontrollably while squeezing and fondling her with a ferocity that made her toss her head backward and scream wantonly. Ethan had never experienced a woman exuding such an orgasmic energy. Her body convulsed in his arms in rippling waves of pleasure. He felt like a knight in shining armor, conquering dark forces in a glorious dark night, to come to prostrate in front of the queen of his heart.

Her beautiful eyes penetrated into the depth of his soul and conveyed a message of love and longing, a surrender of her exquisite feminine to his all-consuming primal maleness. His heart ripped in half, feeling her devotional adoration. He thrust deep into her; he probed every millimeter of her sacred mystery. Ethan plowed into her so hard that he thought, for a blinding second, that he might have split her body in half. He screamed savagely and he felt as if his orgasm could topple the tallest steeple of San Marco square. She held a sensuous space for his torrents of love as he exploded inside of her. When his fire subsided and he came slowly back to consciousness, from God knows where, he heard waltz music drifting by. Ethan realized that he had never given himself to any woman so completely. All the tightness within him and all the problems of the world dissolved away into a tender sweetness. He had never felt such joy of abandon as he did with this exquisitely sexy Madonna. "Who are you? Are you for real?" He asked in trembling ecstasy. "*Sono Venere,*" she responded in sensuous lilting Italian. "Venus—is your name Venus? Or are you Venus of the sea, the love Goddess?!" Ethan exclaimed incredulously. She nodded calmly with an alluring smile. He knew she could instantly disintegrate him into the void with that smile and he would willingly be obliterated into the love that she emanated. The vibrational flickering around her was a translucent golden pink—he was swimming in her aura of unbounded love.

She tenderly rearranged his clothes to give him some decent covering, and then elegantly re-draped her stunning, graceful body with the flowing aqua chiffon. She whispered in English, "You need to catch the last ferry to Lido," kissed him passionately one last time, and then glided effortlessly away. He was planted there, stunned, unable to move, helplessly watching her disappear into the night. He swore he saw her vanish into the deep sea of Venice. In a daze, he managed to find the ferry station and sure enough, he was just minutes away from the ferry's last call for boarding. Ethan looked at his watch: it was 11:11 pm.

While traversing the sea hamlet, he couldn't stop himself from searching the waters, hopelessly willing her to resurface. 'How does she know that I stay at Lido Island? Is she real or is she a figment of my imagination?'

He suddenly remembered that someone had told him long ago that 11:11 was an encoded doorway bridging this world of duality to an inter-dimensional existence. A knowingness sparked inside of him. He knew that his mind might never fully grasp what had happened on this night, but his heart was full. After disembarking the ferry and making the short walk to his hotel, he stumbled into his room and immediately fell into a deep and satisfying sleep. He had been so gloriously loved and nourished.

In a dream that night the Goddess Venus came to him, wearing the same luminous aqua-blue dress, but now she was bejeweled and queenly in glittering magnificence. She appeared with flowing veils about her, floating on an effervescent water vortex and whispered sensuously to him as in a lullaby: "I have come to renew your spirit and re-ignite your passion. Your work has not been in vain, my beloved, and Venice needs you."

Song of the Mermaid

She sang in rapture...
Their love frequencies birthed the ocean alive, abounding with vibrancy inspired by their ecstatic harmonics.

Song of the Mermaid

IT WAS a sunny afternoon when Justin stepped outside. He had just finished attending an international conference on marine biology in the Maldives. He decided to go for a hike around a jagged, rock-strewn beach that some locals had told him about. The path to the beach was quite steep with several twists and turns; no wonder it was of the best-kept secrets in the area. This was a beach where he could swim nude, away from the prying eyes of tourists. Justin was in a good mood and looked forward to some solitary sunbathing and to drinking a couple of cold beers. The glistening beach felt invitingly quiet. As he climbed down the rocky steps, he suddenly saw a reclining figure in the distance that looked like a woman. He felt disappointment; he wanted to claim this private nook for his own, to be alone after days of talking to people. Then he thought, 'what the hell, I can easily share this large haven with another sunbather. We Americans are so spoiled. We feel entitled to our private space wherever we go. Maybe that's why we can't quite relax into being intimate with others.' As he rounded the last rocky turn, to his amazement, the figure seemed to have turned into a sunbathing mermaid, with her shimmering tail flapping playfully on the sand. He rubbed his eyes and quickened his steps with excitement. He vaguely remembered some rumors of mermaid sightings on these islands.

He was quite out of breath when he lurched in front of her. The woman looked up nonchalantly, unperturbed yet with questioning eyes. The translucent sarong covering her beautiful legs fluttered teasingly in the wind, as though mocking his hallucination. Justin felt quite stupid and tongue-tied for mistaking her sarong for a fishtail, and for so rudely intruding upon her quietude. He couldn't take his eyes away from her though—she had an exquisite face with penetrating blue-green eyes, a half-parted sensuous mouth that stirred his imagination, luscious breasts half covered with a bikini top, and a slim waist sculpted with a jewel-like belly button. She softly stretched her long arm to calm her golden hair that was dancing in the wind. His eyes followed the curve of her silky inner arm, which he fantasized caressing right then and there. He dropped to his knees, mesmerized, reverential, in front of such goddess-like splendor.

The woman showed no hint of fear or alarm from his devouring stare. If anything, the way she looked at him seemed to transmit a timeless knowing that resonated with his heart, an elusiveness and familiarity he could not quite grasp. Justin felt locked in a time warp of some tender memory. He was transported to a land of dreams, a place beyond time. Her sensual smile was at once alluring and welcoming. She leisurely unknotted her sarong to reveal long tanned thighs that would drive any man crazy with desire. Her skin-toned bikini shamelessly displayed her like a nude painting, except for those mysterious parts that already overwhelmed his imagination. She half rolled over as though she were getting up; he instinctively reached out and pinned her back down on the sand, his chest protectively embracing hers. His heart was pounding so loudly, he thought he would explode. He had never done anything so bold before!

His hungry eyes searched for further connection as hers melted in his. Furtively, his lips touched her sweet tasting-mouth, his tongue licking its lushness and savoring every tingling sensation. His manhood was now rock hard against her soft belly, while his demanding hand pulled her bikini top down to expose a delicious nipple. His hand and mouth immediately competed to get there first. He bit and suckled her, while savoring her heavenly scent as she uttered fervent moans. His other hand, in one savage grasp, pushed her bikini thong to one side, exposing her glistening Venus mound, while she mischievously made a movement to escape. He rushed to shed his t-shirt and shorts. He was now on his knees, towering above her, straddling her from behind. He slowly breathed in the beauty of her undulating back that glistened with beads of sunlit sand. Using one hand, he rubbed lusciously between her two breasts; waves of craving shot through his body. He arched his back and in veneration licked her rosy vulva, which sparked cries of pleasure from her. He adored how her rose petals mysteriously blossomed into layers of juicy beckoning that drove him even wilder; he turned into a ravenous beast as he drove himself hard inside of her, thrusting and riding her with raw power, intoxicated by her fragrance. He burst into an orgasmic roar when he heard her scream out a rapturous cry of ecstasy. He collapsed onto her but instinctively rolled to her side to protect her from the hot sand, enfolding her tenderly in a spooning position. Their breaths rose and fell in harmonious cadence and they blissfully merged as one.

Some time passed and she stirred, and his aching heart wanted her again. Somewhat satiated from their previous lovemaking, Justin took his time to sensuously feel her skin, so creamy and moist under his caressing fingers. He titillated the delectable textures of her body as she purred and sighed with every nuance of his embrace. A part of him was astonished at how all this happened so naturally, without the slightest hint of resistance from her— this goddess of love whose name he didn't even know.

Women told him he was desirable, and he could get laid quite casually if he wanted to, but this experience was different from all the others. There was a sense of purity and rightness about it that wasn't there in any of his previous flings. There was a sense of magnetic mystery, as if he knew her from somewhere long ago. Strangely, he wanted to love and nurture this delicate orchid curled inside his arms. He dotingly turned her head to face his as he tenderly started to explore the silky fullness of her lips. He drank in the adoring gaze from her fathomless eyes, as though they had always been together. His heartstrings tugged again, his exploring fingers tremulous on her supple skin—every line, every curve, every contour was a sculptor's dream. No matter how he stroked or probed, every inch of her whispered surrender. She had yet to utter a single word, but her body spoke to him with a language of love he had never known before. She returned his caresses, resonating with excitement and yielding in delight.

Justin felt urgent for her again, love and lust merging into a wave of roaring fire. As he cupped her breasts with both of his hands, bringing the glistening nipples to his mouth, his inflamed rod naturally searched for the entrance to her velvety mound, but it bumped up against a slippery sensation that felt unfamiliar, yet luscious. He looked down, and in one dizzying shock he saw that his legs were wrapped around a splendidly colored half-fish with a twirl of a florescent tail. He dazedly looked up and her gorgeous face took on a forlorn begging for understanding. A huge tear sparkled on her left cheek. Justin swiftly sprang up to steady her swaying body, which was slipping away from him. He had no clue why he wasn't repulsed or terrified; maybe because that was how he spotted her to begin with—a woman with a fish tail, or maybe there rang a far-away memory of mermaid love that was appealing to him.

He started to form a question but her delicate finger softly silenced his mouth. In wave-like patterns, she communicated telepathically to him to go with her. With one graceful twirl of her arm, entwined with his, she glided both of them into the water. Effortlessly and lithely, they plunged into the depths of the ocean layers. While his logical mind was warning him he needed a tank of oxygen to do such a dive, his trusting mind already knew that they could do this together, as though they were one body and one soul. Every pore in his body was overjoyed with knowing, freedom, and liberation, loving the exhilarating waters that propelled them onward through tumbling sensuous funnels.

The panorama unfurling in front of them was an enchanted heaven beyond words. Justin had yet to experience the deep waters of the Maldives. All around them were beautiful mermaids frolicking with their human lovers who looked enthralled and ecstatic. Captivated, Justin witnessed in awe the expressions of devotion that emanated from the mermaids as they sang in rapturous tones. The ocean responded and came alive as though there was a magical wand from a symphony conductor guiding a magnificent ensemble. The corals burst open in dazzling glamour, the colorful sea plants moved in serpentine exotic whirls, and a thousand schools of scintillating fish fanned out like peacocks with rainbow radiance. Rock grottoes breathed sighs of joy and stretched out their wondrous formations as octopuses wiggled in their seductive, manifold dance.

The glory of this cornucopia, bursting with so much life force, brought hot tears to Justin's eyes. This was why he loved to go diving years ago; the mystical grandeur and mysterious water world was a wonder to behold. He watched with complete absorption as his beautiful *Lorelei* sang in exquisite high-pitched tones that electrified the waters. Her hands were folded in devotional poise over her breasts and heart. Her tail undulated in green, gold, and silver luminescence, splashing waves of crystal foam around her. She was surrounded by adoring sea creatures and trance-dancing seaweeds. Justin came to an epiphany in that moment which helped him fathom the mystery of the millennia about mermaids. They have been here for eons to sing the oceans alive with love frequencies that birthed a multitude of life forms. The mermaids welcomed their human lovers by their sides to enliven their sexual nectars. This inspired their mutual ecstatic harmonics that stirred the cauldron of life on this majestic planet of water.

In one omniscient gasp, he understood the tales and lies, born from religious and patriarchal fear, which made these beautiful beings into evil seductresses and men-swallowing nymphs. In reality, the men who loved these beings volunteered their sacred mating for this glorious fire of co-creation, in order to bring bountiful life to our planet for eternity. No wonder so many of these men never came back to land, they were elated to be in such devotional service to life itself! Jubilantly, Justin joined his beloved and sang with her in exaltation, clasping her hand with veneration and love. In that moment their spirits merged as one. Everyone around them ardently chanted in chorus. The deep male resonance complemented the exquisite high female tones, fueling the power of the ocean's might. The whales responded, emanating their potent vibrations to penetrate and stabilize the depths of the Earth, while the undulating dolphins squealed in wisdom's exuberant dance.

Flashes of memories began to resurface, Justin now remembered the many incarnations in which he had joined with his beloved. No wonder he wasn't the least bit afraid when his beauty beckoned him to follow her into the water. No wonder he longed to go diving ever since he was a young boy. He had always been searching for something so splendid and elusive that even in the midst of diving in the most stunning oceans of the world, he was still left yearning. Maybe that was why he rarely dived anymore in recent years; he was aching to reunite with his long lost love without knowing it consciously.

As he dreamily recalled the mysterious layers of his soul's knowing, she ever so fluidly pulled him back up onto the shimmering sand. Now he was chin-to-chin with his precious love, as she caressed his whole body with grateful worship through her dancing hands. She looked more radiant than before, as if that was possible! He now recognized her familiar scent and the feelings expressed in her eyes that he so adored. They had been together for many lifetimes. 'Mermaid or human— does it matter when there is infinite love?' Justin thought tenderly.

Still nestled in his warm embrace, she languidly turned away, facing the ocean, leaning on him gracefully with her tail splashing in the waters. She pulled his hands away from her waist and onto her breasts, placing his fingers at the base of each of them. She guided him to alternately squeeze hard and fondle her nipples. He excitedly flicked his nails on their tips, which thrilled her to screams of euphoria. He was beyond intoxicated by her pleasure. Her erotic moans made him hard again. He wanted her so badly that he would do anything to split her tail open, so his burning steed could fill her up again. As though reading his mind, she turned her head ever so slightly toward him with longing eyes that inspired his heart. He slid hard up and down, behind her fish buttocks, willing with all his might to tear asunder the shimmering scales. He quickened his squeezes and pulled her juicy breasts in a frenzied tempo, like inebriating drumbeats.

Suddenly, copious sprays of a milky elixir shot out of her nipples. Simultaneously, huge ocean waves lashed onto jagged rocks, splashing dancing foam. She cried out such an earth-shattering orgasm that the crystalline echoes reverberated throughout the whole enclave. In that moment his electrified wand felt flesh. He looked down, expectant yet flabbergasted. His shaft had now disappeared inside her, at home with the most blissful sensation a man could ever feel. Scales and tail vanished; the power of his love had transformed her lower body into wide-open legs. He went wild throbbing inside of her, fully engulfed by wanton desire, thrusting forcefully into her depths. Both of them, now in standing positions, became one dizzying dervish whirl. He exploded in a rock-splitting roar so primal that flocks of birds spontaneously shot up in a fan-like rainbow pantheon across the sky. In that moment Justin felt as ecstatic as the King of Kings, having brought his beloved back into full womanhood. It was divine rapture beyond words.

He pulled her down ever so reverently to lie with him on the golden sand, kissing her hair and her coral lips. A magnificent sunset inundated the land as a grand finale, celebrating their bliss. She looked deep into his soul with gratitude and bid him farewell with adoration and the promise of love in her tear-filled emerald eyes. Justin did not resist the imminent parting; he knew in the bottomless whirl of his heart that she was devoted to the ocean. Justin also knew they would be together again and again, journeying through dimensions of parallel realities, either in the netherworld or the ocean world. This love had made him a better man. His heart was awakened and he no longer needed to ache for the mysterious tenderness that had haunted him his whole life. He watched her half roll, half glide away toward the horizon against the luminescent shards of sunset glory. Oh, how he loved to watch her graceful back. Her indelible imprint seared in his heart the knowing that he would recognize her anywhere or anyplace.

As he reluctantly relinquished her presence, he watched, through bittersweet tears streaming down his face, as she came up on a rock with a graceful flip of her sensual tail. A larger-than-life swan swooped down from the sky with a luminous dragonfly poised on top of its left wing. "Swans fly through dreamtimes," Justin heard his beloved whisper through the wind, "the power of woman entering sacred space, touching future yet to come, bringing eternal grace."[1] He knew that. She always brought a variation of this poetic notion to him in her many moods, disguises, and incarnations, while manifesting a dragonfly each time to remind him of mystical magic. He remembered it so well—its elusive wings of transcendence are doorways to all planes of imagination.

---

1. Jamie Sams and David Carson, *The Medicine Cards* (New York: St. Martin's, 1999), 192.

In Guan Yin's Rapture

Levitated into a tantric entwinement,
he was enthralled by her gaze of love
—filled with kindness and sensual purity.

In Guan Yin's Rapture

BLAKE felt he had been running in circles for over two weeks now. He was in the city of Suzhou—coined as the Silicon Valley of China due to the flourishing of high-tech companies there, trying to train a group of unruly middle management staff on the principles of 21st century leadership models. He was the global director of talent development for a multinational corporation based in Los Angeles. Blake had been on the road to several countries heading up this training; little did he know that the office in China would be the most challenging one to date, with the toughest staff. His previous interactions with the Chinese were generally quite cordial, but somehow everything seemed to have changed in the last two years. They had become brassy, with a 'we-are-smarter-than-you-round-eyes' kind of attitude—rebellious and a bit scornful of almost anything he had to impart. A number of translators and business mediators had been called in for assistance, but to his frustration, their interpretations of his training materials always led to more confusion. He had enough international experience to know that many of the concepts he introduced were lost in translation.

Several days ago, a new interpreter was sent in. Her

name was Ci-Ai. Her mature confidence and disarmingly soft demeanor won over the staff rather quickly. People started to be more attentive and receptive. She had a master's degree in organizational management from a stateside university. She had previously worked in the United States for quite a few years, and her English was excellent. She seemed totally at ease bridging the two cultures. Blake finally relaxed for the first time and was hopeful that the training would go well from this point on. Ci-Ai was an attractive woman and her manners were reserved and dignified. Her hair was always pulled back in a bun, as though wanting to give off a more serious aura than her petite frame could convey. Besides respecting her effectiveness with the group, Blake felt quite an attraction toward her. He noticed that she didn't wear a wedding ring. A few times he wanted to invite her out for dinner to thank her for her competency with the group, but either shyness or some kind of ego competitiveness prevented him from doing so. He liked to be in control of things and wanted to ascertain energetically that he was the one in charge, though she was obviously the one who was making things work.

Tonight Blake was in his hotel room, feeling bored.

There was only so much sightseeing he could handle, even though Suzhou was a beautiful city. It was famous for its meandering canals, hand-embroidered art, and stunning architecture. Hundreds of years ago, in Beijing, the emperor of the first Qing Dynasty had ordered shiploads of architects, designers and craftsmen from Suzhou to help build the spectacular Forbidden City as the imperial palace. Blake also could only take so much solo drinking in bars or flirting with seductive young women who sported Pidgin English. Business travels in a foreign country can get quite lonely; it's not as glamorous as people think. He dozed off after watching a bit of depressing news on CNN, drifting into slumber.

In a somewhat lucid dream state, Blake saw a woman come to him in veils of translucent white. Guan Yin—the Chinese Goddess of Love and Compassion, enfolded in sensually flowing silk—looked deeply into him with her limpid almond-shaped eyes, surrounding him with a whirling vortex of love. She smiled at him through her rose-colored lips, which were perfectly framed between her delicate nose and her slightly upward tilting chin. She looked like Ci-Ai, whom Blake didn't dare to stare at during work. Now she was in full display, right there for him to admire at his leisure. Her long neck was sensuous. The plunging silky folds of her dress exposed her bare shoulder, revealing lustrous, silky skin. Her long black hair was free flowing. It danced about her, with strands of pearls and wispy ribbons laced through it, which enhanced her mysterious beauty.

She delicately came upon him, bestriding him with grace and self-assuredness. The silhouette of her breasts, with nipples hard and plump, beckoned from behind the silk that hugged her bodylines. This triggered an agonizing yearning in Blake. The subtle temptation of her veiled, small, firm breasts drove him wild with desire. He wanted her desperately, but he was a bit intimidated. After all, she was Guan Yin—*The Goddess* of the Chinese culture, did he dare trespass? But she was so alluringly inviting.

She started trance dancing from her waist up, humming sensually celestial tones in a never-heard-of-before high frequency. It soothed his ears sublimely, like flowing crystalline water, transporting him into realms of exaltation. First he started touching her tentatively, then in appreciative slow motion. Her long, slim fingers responded with languid strokes through the hair of his torso, playing with him teasingly. Enchanted, Blake proceeded from probing her soft, silky arm to grabbing her lustily. He raised himself part way up to caress her exquisite shoulder blade with his lips. He playfully undressed her with his teeth, one filmy veil at a time, gradually revealing her soft and juicy breasts, like ripe peaches begging to be bitten into. The tiny glands of her areola were so erect and lusciously excited that he could spend hours just worshipping this pair of coral jewels. They were taunting him to take it all into his mouth, which he savored deliriously. Every exploding sensation on his tongue drove him euphorically into inebriated pleasure.

Still moving in slow motion, they now levitated into a sitting tantric entwinement on an enormous lotus leaf floating on clouds in heavenly surroundings, with lotuses blooming all around them in shades of pink and red. Her transparent clothing quivered in the wind, revealing her goddess mound. Blake was in complete ecstasy in front of such magnificence. He instinctively bowed his head as if in prostration; bliss and gratitude overwhelmed him in the presence of so much loving energy. Her hand caressed his hair, titillating all his senses, and she languorously fingered the contour of his handsomely chiseled face. He looked up and met her gaze of love. Passion and compassion were united in that exquisite wanton smile, which seemed beyond the human realm. How was it possible that she possessed such amorous purity, kindness, and sensuality all at once so effortlessly?

She shifted her thighs ever so gracefully to reveal the almost imperceptible shy folds of her labia, bewitching him to explore. He lost all restraint and reservation. His tongue slowly, yet passionately, twirled inside of her nectar, as if his whole being was whirled into a cyclone of love eternal. His nostrils were filled with the pristine aroma of dewdrops mixed with the rich perfume of her womanhood. Blake reveled in tasting the entrancing layers of her velvety softness. His tongue probed deeper, subconsciously yearning to find that elusive G-spot, which myth and science competed to expose within a woman's body. He was more intoxicated than any of Rumi's ecstatic poems could ever convey. He looked up adoringly and watched her moan blissfully. With one hand in his hair, she used the other to pull him closer to her bosom. Trance-like he rose, his inflamed phallus deliriously wanting her. While his eyes followed the sensual contour of her half-parted lips, he slid inside her fluidly, as though they had been mating forever. The erotic energy between them was beyond anything Blake had ever experienced with any woman. Raw sexuality, fused with tenderness, radiated through every pore of their beings. A simultaneous cry of shattering exultation tore through the air, pierced through the stars, and exploded in rings of glory throughout the Universe. He was annihilated into the oblivion of infinite love. He always knew in his heart that he could love and adore a woman like this. His love and lust encounters thus far in life always fell short of the transcendence he was subconsciously searching for—the all-encompassing bliss he had just now experienced. There was nothing a man wouldn't do for a woman he could love with such abandon!

As their passion subsided into a calm sea of tender sweetness, holding and softly caressing each other, she thoughtfully laid Blake's head back onto the pillow of his hotel bed. She gradually faded into a perfumed cloud behind a shroud of interstellar music, a sublime vision beyond anything he'd ever beheld. With a divine smile filled with love, she dreamily waved to him with one hand, while the other sprinkled a heavenly mist on him from her vase of eternal water, as if anointing him. His body sprang alive, tingling with wanting still.

On one side of Guan Yin, Blake saw a devout boy-man who stood on a lotus with hands together in fervent prayer. He looked with adoration into the eyes of his counterpart, a girl-woman also standing upon a lotus on the other side of Guan Yin, reflecting the posture of the boy. She looked back with devotion into her companion's eyes. The trinity emanated such an aura of brilliant light that Blake's heart opened wide and he luxuriated in its radiance.

Suddenly Blake woke up disoriented, still hearing the celestial melody in his room; a waft of aromatic elixir lingered. He jerked up from his bed but no one was there. Was he really dreaming? Guan Yin's presence was so real and palpable just a while ago. His body was satiated; he could still feel her warmth on him when he drifted into a deep sleep.

Blake went to work the next day, dazed yet trembling with excitement to see Ci-Ai. She was already there, casually chatting with a few workers who had arrived early. As he approached the glass door of the conference room, he purposely slowed his steps to drink her in. Today she was in a white outfit—what a coincidence! She was not in her usual pantsuit, but wore a silk top with a flowing half-lotus-leaf collar and a slim three-quarter length skirt that sensually revealed her beautiful contours. The back of her skirt was adorned with a few buttons in the middle that started from below her buttocks and ended on a long slit that flirtatiously swayed as she moved. This was the first time she wore a skirt that so flattered her gorgeous legs on high-heeled sandals. She didn't wear any stockings and the silky tan of her skin was temptingly mouth-watering. Blake's heart was bursting with desire.

He got a cup of tea so he would have something in his hand to steady his nerves. He mustered the courage to move toward her as casually as he could and said, "Good morning." The boyish excitement in his voice betrayed his calm exterior. She stopped what she was doing and slightly turned her head toward him. "You are in a good mood today, did you dream of me last night?" she asked with a glint in her smiling eyes. There was no malice or seduction in her tone, just pure delight. Blake was so shocked by the directness of her question, that all he could do was look at her, dumbfounded. He noticed an almost imperceptible quiver above the right corner of her upper lip that betrayed her own excitement and nervousness.

Blake moved through his workday dreamily. His

whole comportment was softened by the beautiful encounter he had last night. He didn't remember how he got through the day—what he or anyone else said, but somehow the day went perfectly, without discord or argument. Everyone at the office was lighthearted. There was a pleasant atmosphere of camaraderie and team spirit. The staff discussed more openly the different cultural points of view about leadership and Blake truly listened for the first time. An objective part of him observed all of this in a stunned realization that unity like this could be effortless. It was his best day yet with this group and he didn't even have to try too hard.

Blake's eyes followed Ci-Ai all day long. There wasn't a bone of resistance in him and he felt no need to safeguard his *in-charge* persona. He appraised her with agreement and delight as she took over the presentation; the room melted into a joyous harmony. He felt a change had taken hold of him. His heart relaxed into a considerate appreciation of each person's opinion as he interacted with the group. He was humbled by the occurrences of the day. It was clear now that so many of the challenges in the past weeks were projections of his own ego, his own arrogant judgment of the differences between the East and the West. He realized his earlier competitiveness toward Ci-Ai came from his own insecurity and his self-perceived importance. After being so generously loved last night by Guan Yin, all the previous tension he felt seemed like such a meaningless vanity.

As everyone said their goodbyes and happily shuffled out of the room around 6 pm, a young man and a woman came up to Blake to tell him, in halting English, how much they enjoyed his teaching. He genuinely gave them a pat on the back and told them he looked forward to tomorrow. Wow, what happened? What changed? Everything went so easily and congenially. Was it just because the Goddess had loved him in his dream? He approached Ci-Ai and thanked her for the great day. She looked up amidst her folders of documents, smiled broadly at him in acknowledgment, then mumbled something about still having a lot of pages to translate and she returned to her papers. He wanted to explore the daring question that she had raised at the beginning of the day, when she asked if he dreamed of her, but he couldn't rudely interrupt her work. He lamely asked whether she needed him to hang around and answer any questions. "Indeed," she replied positively without the faintest of pretention, and they harmoniously went to work.

Blake suddenly noticed that the staff was all gone and they were alone in the silent office, save for the humming of a few machines. All the lights were dimmed except in the conference room where they were working. The office workers must have been sensitive to not disturb them when they left, since they knew that Blake had the keys to lock up. He was excited at this opportunity to be alone with her. He thought of asking her to share a meal with him. As if reading his mind, Ci-Ai put down her pen, came close to him and tenderly asked, "Are you wondering how best to spend the evening with me?" Once again, astounded by her psychic ability, he blurted out, "Are you a mind reader?" She half-smiled modestly and looked at him lovingly. She didn't answer, but sat down facing him, her dancing eyes appraising his body. His imagination went wild and he impulsively grabbed the back of her head, pulling her toward him swiftly.

Blake laced his fingers through her luxurious hair, ruffling her impeccable bun, and kissed her passionately. He was hungry to taste her mouth—he didn't get to last night—and she returned his craving with a long, enticing kiss. Their tongues entwined, exploring each other in slow motion and then urgently. He fumbled to caress her everywhere, starving for those ambrosial breasts again. With one savage yank of her blouse, he needed to know if they were exactly how he felt, experienced and loved them less than twenty hours ago—small and firm, exquisite and juicy like ripe peaches, which he voraciously bit into. He was once again transported to the heights of ecstasy.

He had fantasized about undressing her from the back of her skirt all day. With both of his hands on her sinuous waist, he powerfully turned her over on the conference table. With her bottom propped up, he immediately wanted to tear off her skirt, which was clinging tightly to her curves. Unexpectedly, Blake's slow motion dream of last night came to life. He took a deep breath to calm his roaring fire, remembering Guan Yin's sublime presence again. First he slowly took off his shirt, and then he deliberately unbuttoned her skirt, while his other hand leisurely moved between the silkiness of her inner thighs and up the curves of her back, which were so delicate that his heart ached with adoration. Ci-Ai then slowly guided his hand to flutter between her two breasts as she arched up from the table.

Her hair was now loosened from the bun and

splashed across her back; this was incredibly sexy to him. She half-turned her head around to gaze at him; that same gaze of infinite love bestowed upon him by Guan Yin last night. His mouth rushed to meet hers, to taste her sweet tongue once again. Their bodies undulated together, skin-to-skin, rubbing each other erotically as their groaning sparked a blazing desire in both of them. As he flicked open the last button and pushed up her skirt, he delicately caressed her private jewel—a rosy sight so splendid that he just went crazy with wanting. He tantalized her delicious layers and then slowly savored her elixir. A bursting fire emanated throughout his body.

Ci-Ai gracefully flipped around to face him. Her stunning half-covered body was tremulous; sensuality oozed out of her every pore. She deliberately undid his belt and unbuttoned his pants, while her other hand caressed his bulge erotically. He stood engorged, his purple-blooded steed anticipating more. She drank in the vision of him and then lithely inserted him inside her rose gate. They tumbled into a nirvana of carnal recklessness, flying through fantastical realms of exploding lusciousness. His intense desire and overwhelming passion were so met by her that he never wanted to come back into ho-hum existence. They both shot out such cries of pleasure that he thought the glass walls of the conference room would come thundering down, just as his rumbling heart shattered in a thousand jubilant smithereens.

Ci-Ai relaxed with a blossom of a smile on her face. Her breasts glistened with sweat, her hair flew about like billowing wind, and her heart pulsed in noticeable cadences. He was still inside of her, throbbing at the edge of the table, straddling her beautiful bare legs. She looked tranquil and poised, and very much like Guan Yin. He bent down to massage her body with his tongue admiringly, bewitched by her delicious curves. He took hold of her left knee and felt its smooth hollows, with his fingers drumming and rising slowly along her thigh. They felt so complete in each other that tears of joy streamed out simultaneously from their eyes. They adored each other in silence; no words were needed. This wasn't the first time Blake had office sex encounters with which he usually felt his ego stroked and lust gratified. Why was this time so exquisitely different? Was it because of the transcendent influence of last night, or the result of their rapturous lovemaking just now?

Blake commented to Ci-Ai how beautifully uninhibited she was. She shyly confided she had never done anything like it before, but that a force guided her beyond her mind. He then softly asked her how she knew about his dream of the night before. "It wasn't a dream, my darling, I came to love you. There seems to be an urgency propelled by my soul to reconnect with you," she whispered tenderly as though they had always known each other, acknowledging her astral visit without a hint of arrogance, as if it were a normal occurrence for her. She then thoughtfully continued, "People all over the world blindly worship Guan Yin as an icon of love and compassion, but never question whether she has sexual desires. If she didn't personify the exquisiteness of sex, how could she preside as *The Goddess of Love?*" She went on to say that there was the same puritanism in the East as well as the West. Humanity was only comfortable worshipping Mother Mary as the pure Madonna, and Guan Yin as the Love Goddess as long as there was no reference to sexual union. Blake never thought of that before but he couldn't agree more.

Blake asked inquiringly, "What does Guan Yin really mean?" Ci-Ai responded: "Her full name is *Guan Shi*

Yin. It carries layers of connotations and it essentially means the *One* who contemplates the troubled cries of the world—she hears the sufferings of all beings." This explanation roused his curiosity even further and he wanted to know more. "Guan Yin is not just a Goddess for the Chinese; she embodies the ultimate feminine energy of creation, and is called by many different names in Asian cultures. She incarnates in a female body, in all shapes and forms through the ages, to help liberate humanity from the perpetually pain-filled cycles of birth, death, and rebirth. She has vowed to remain and serve in the earthly realms through infinite disguises until all living beings attain their own enlightenment. She is the quintessence of divine selfless love and compassion. You can say that she is a manifestation of Mother Earth herself, tirelessly caring for all of her children." Though some of what she said flew over his head, he now appreciated more fully the magnitude of Guan Yin, his dream lover of last night.

"What about the young couple who accompanied her?" Blake inquired further. She smiled at him and illuminated him with delight: "They are the legendary *Golden Boy* and *Jade Maiden*, and a pair of lovers who journey eternally with Guan Yin wherever she goes.

They are love united—twin souls in male and female embodiments of sacred union. They are here to remind us that ultimately, everything in life is about love. They are Yin and Yang in perfect harmony, a heart space beyond duality."

Ci-Ai half-raised her body to snuggle into his. "You are the *Golden Boy*," she ruffled his blond hair and adoringly said, "I'm the *Jade Maiden*." He returned her loving look and plumbed the depths of her dark brown eyes, which swirled in unfathomable pools of translucent jade. Blake was confused, "But I thought you were Guan Yin?" She sealed his lips with hers and whispered with innocent conviction, "Yes, I'm an aspect of her cosmic energy making love with the divine light in you to awaken your soul. But in mortal life, we are the twin soul lovers who have a sublime mission toward humanity." Ci-Ai said she recognized his soul from the spark in his eyes the first time she met him. She seemed to have no trouble living in different realms of reality and making enigmatic statements. She didn't offer further explanation on how she astral-traveled and transformed into Guan Yin. He grappled to understand but he was too enthralled in the moment to be mental about magic.

The next few weeks flew by in a blur. Blake was so in love he didn't know how he was able to function normally at work, though the training was completed successfully. He had learned a lot from Ci-Ai how to sensitively handle ethnic differences and how to give respect to others' philosophies and business traditions before conceitedly injecting his views and principles—a common mistake made by Westerners in other countries, assuming that the world should follow their ethics and ideologies, without probing deeper into others' cultural values.

Blake also rejoiced how he and Ci-Ai spent the enchanted evenings and weekends together. They were either in her tastefully decorated small apartment, where she continued to educate him about Guan Yin and cooked up appetizing local delicacies for dinner, or they lingered in his hotel room making exquisite love. He finally got the opportunity to discover her many facets. He noticed how he softened to listen attentively to her upon the joy of their sexual bliss. He was humbled to learn so much from her quiet wisdom; to learn about her dedication to her country and her culture.

She had a difficult childhood. Her parents were factory laborers and both died of lung cancer when

Ci-Ai was very young. She was subsequently passed around from town to town, to live with various relatives. Her sub-standard living environs built her strength and character. Ci-Ai persevered through enormously painful obstacles and worked hard to literally raise herself and her younger relatives. She subsequently got a government scholarship, due to her excellent grades, to pursue her post-graduate studies in the United States. She later gave up a lucrative job in America and returned to China to help her own people, not only with language and other skills, but most importantly, to influence their consciousness in caring about environmental issues. Her previous adversity and sorrows in life made her a more loving and compassionate person. She knew that China was becoming a world superpower. It hurt her deeply to witness the blind greed and out-of-control economic development of its government, heavily influenced by its own monopolistic giants and foreign corporations, at the expense of the people and the precious planet. She felt someday the country would implode upon itself if people like her were too selfish, jaded, or lazy to do something about it.

In her view, global power comes with an even

higher responsibility toward humankind. Ci-Ai had made a commitment to herself to help enlighten the masses, even if her efforts only impacted one person at a time. She had been tirelessly volunteering her time for causes that uplift humanity and that teach sustainability to the young generations. She had faith in the inherent kindness of the Chinese people, whose DNA carries the signature of the way of the *Tao* that reveres nature. She also revealed that Guan Yin had always been her omniscient protector and her Oversoul, guiding her to pledge herself as an embodiment of selfless love. 'Indeed her life choices parallel those of Guan Yin,' Blake reflected with admiration. He could see how much her inner values illuminated her outer beauty.

As his departure date neared, Blake implored Ci-Ai to move back to the states with him. He yearned to have this beautiful relationship in his daily life. He knew that she could easily find a suitable job with all her skills and talents. "It's not just a job that I want. You know that I have a sacred duty toward humanity. I'm a bridge between East and West to unite our forces together in peace for the evolution of consciousness, not in opposition or competition with one another. My work needs to be inspired by a calling." On a personal level, she was already doing a fine job. Blake was a man transformed by her love.

"When you are ready to embark on a divine journey with me, I'll come to you," she promised brightly, with patience and trust in her eyes. He couldn't quite assimilate all her cryptic words, but he somehow intuited their meaning. He knew their love was ultimately for a higher purpose than for mere personal cocooning and gratification. After all, her name was Ci-Ai, which meant *Loving Compassion.* She was an aspect of Guan Yin incarnated; she could manifest anything. Blake didn't have to know about their future; he was confident her spirit would motivate him and guide him to the next chapter unfolding in his life. For the first time, he didn't feel the need to control everything; he relaxed into a sweet acceptance of the unknown.

Blake wasn't overly depressed when they said goodbye at the Shanghai airport. She fondly held his face, her serene silence promising love and reunion with a tenderness that gave him strength; then he boarded the aircraft. As he looked out the window of the departing plane, he fantasized her running toward him, as in a romantic movie. Then he smiled to himself with a calm happiness, knowing that he was at long last united with the love of his life. His heart was now committed to a beautiful woman with an invincible spirit and a passionate, tender nature.

Blake felt that he was a changed man. He realized that traveling around the world to develop talents in others was ultimately his own quest for his innate gift to connect between realms of realities and to discover their mysteries. His dream encounter with Guan Yin had altered him in some fundamental way. It was the sublime opening of his soul beyond an erotic happenstance that led him to his true love, and that gave him a new perspective on his place in the world. Blake felt alive and bursting with purpose for the first time in his life. He was being interwoven into a bridge between East and West, conjoining philosophies and cultures, uniting hearts with love and compassion. The divine feminine has now become a guiding light in his life. His future with his beloved seemed elusive, yet he never felt more certain and fulfilled.

The Temple Dancer

Undulating to the sound of flutes and tambourines,
she danced with burning passion,
embodying desire, regeneration and creation itself.

The Temple Dancer

IT WAS late Saturday evening. Gabriel, a freelance photographer who worked for a few well-known national magazines, had just arrived home the day before after a rather long assignment in France. His neighbor Chris brought over beer and pizza to hang out with him, share some weed, and shoot the breeze. They lived in the cozy neighborhood of North Beach, the *Little Italy* of San Francisco. Gabriel was pleasantly buzzed; he sprawled out on the floor to relax and shake off his jet-lag drowsiness. Chris suggested later that they mosey down Broadway to check out some girly bars. Gabriel was not into strip joints; he didn't care to frequent them, even in exotic locations during his travels. He was the rather idealistic type and didn't condone nor care for that kind of entertainment. But he was somewhat listless tonight, so he agreed, welcoming the distraction. Chris seemed to know his way around the seedy area of downtown Broadway, on the other side of Chinatown, where blinking neon signs of nude women and sleazy pimps competed to lure in anyone who even cast a glance at the assortment of erotic posters pasted all over the walls of glitzy bars.

Chris led the way into a rather tastefully decorated

topless bar where some pole dancers were gyrating seductively on stage. Men of various nationalities ogled and whistled; ready every chance they got to slip dollar bills into the dancers' tantalizing thongs. Chris mumbled something about lap dancing and steered Gabriel to the backside of the bar. Before he knew what was happening, Gabriel was seated in a cushioned, tall-backed chair in a small room with lush velvety walls and dim lighting. A foxy woman came in with a couple of drinks and Chris whispered in her ear. He then told Gabriel he was treating him to a private dance performance. Chris winked at him to enjoy it before disappearing with the woman. Gabriel just went along, not knowing what to expect, since he had never experienced a lap dance before.

Melancholic Middle Eastern music began playing and an exotically clad woman entered the room, her face half-veiled behind a chiffon scarf held up by her bejeweled fingers. Her piercing eyes were stunning, gazing at him with an erotic intensity. She was attired like a belly dancer with a glimmering beaded bra that augmented her breasts, which were tightly pressed together. Her clothing was not the cheap costume of a street girl, but an ensemble of exquisite taste. Gabriel appreciatively assessed her beauty and dreamily framed her in different angles with his photographic mind. Through his hazily stoned eyes, she looked like a Persian princess; her flowing saffron skirt was decorated with lovely trims in flattering colors. Aesthetically placed ornaments adorned her luscious black hair, her long neck, and her slender arms. Gabriel had always been partial to Middle Eastern costumes; they evoked the exotic mysteries of the *Tales of the Arabian Nights*. He thought to himself, 'how did Chris know my taste?' Without any exchange of greetings, the dancer confidently straddled him and started to twirl suggestively to the melody. Gabriel sighed contently and leaned back to enjoy the ride. Without preambles or warnings, he was suddenly transported to an ancient time, as he peered into the golden pools of her mesmerizing eyes.

Gabriel saw himself garbed in a warrior's elaborate costume. He had just come back from war, after months on the battlefield. He impatiently dismounted from his horse and rushed through a temple courtyard. Goddess worship was evident everywhere, in life-size statues and in exquisite carvings on huge pillars. Flower petals were strewn about, aromatic incense drifted by like wispy clouds, trance-like fires blazed from stately golden urns, and temple dancers in sensual veils undulated worshipfully to the sound of flutes and the rousing rhythms of tambourines. They danced with burning passion, embodying desire, creation, vitality and regeneration as Earth goddesses.

The warrior anxiously moved through the swaying bodies to look for the lover he always came to visit after battles. In a far corner he saw her whirling in joyous abandon, her graceful fingers arrayed in reverential mudras. He rushed to her and their eyes met; she fell into his arms with delight and surprised excitement. Her beauty and the purity of her sensuality brought tears to his eyes, which melted his heart every time. Without a word, she gently led him to her chamber, deftly took off his heavy armor, and tenderly probed for scars and wounds, while a couple of attendants hurried off to prepare a hot bath. She bathed him with deliberate care, using fresh marigold flowers and medicinal herbs to rejuvenate him. She tended to the injured areas with her healing hands, all the while adoring him with her eyes. All his stress and strain dissolved away as she laid him down on soft cushions of her bed. Attendants lit oil lamps, creating a sensuous ambience before they quietly glided out of the private quarters.

While softly humming a chant, which was soothing to his ears, she gently bestrode him and started to erotically peel off her filmy clothes in languid movements. She swayed provocatively as she dabbed sandalwood and bergamot oils around her breasts, on her inner thighs, and on the lips of her sacred mound. He was deliriously aroused and he was desperate to possess her. Her teasing eyes welcomed his lust and expressed how much she yearned for him too. Her rhythm was graceful and provocative. She moved with an elegant certainty of owning her feminine power. She lowered her body and kissed him with unrestrained passion, while rubbing herself suggestively on his chest in a way that thrilled him. His whole body was agonizingly on fire; he could not wait a moment longer. He needed to deeply penetrate her in body and in spirit. He grabbed her hungrily and entered her with the force of an erupting volcano, unleashing all his pent-up desires and anguish. She tauntingly pushed up hard against him and they tumbled through ecstatic and lashing waves of euphoria.

He surrendered and released all the repressed feelings of the months of nightmarish atrocities and intoxicating victories. He let flow all the tears he couldn't shed for the innocent lives taken in the name of defending the land and the kingdom that he had pledged his life to. Their sacred mating had always been the pinnacle of his redemption. Their sexual rapture was the summit of their united prayer for divine forgiveness to the perpetual cycles of wars and bloodsheds. She offered him immeasurable solace and revitalized him. She mystically embodied heavenly bliss and grounded earthiness. In her arms he felt safe to break down in sorrowful tears like an innocent child, baring his vulnerability in the consoling folds of her understanding strokes. They laughed and cried together as he told her story after story. There was a magic about her that soothed and rejuvenated his heart and soul.

Her adoring response to him and her compassionate kindness enraptured him from the first time he laid eyes on her; since then he felt an enduring love for her. But she did not belong to him. She belonged to the Temple of Love, where she willingly served with her sexual ecstasy. She danced for the unbounded life of the Divine Feminine, for Mother Earth and all her sentient beings. She and her fellow temple dancers were the most liberated people he had ever known, even freer than men in any strata of power. These maidens abided only by the divine laws of sovereignty in sacred union and not by any conventional mores. Her passionate lovemaking and tender care bespoke love and devotion, but she made no demands on him whatsoever. She lived in the moment, serving him with all her heart and body, though at times he saw the tears that she fiercely tried to hold back behind a wistful smile when they bid farewell.

Warriors traditionally came to the temples to offer their battle-worn bodies in spirit and love to the Goddess—the Ancient Mother energy that coiled at the origin of all of creations. They entrusted themselves to the dancing maidens, whose lives were devoted to the service of healing, without compensation, through the honorable act of erotic passion. In this sacred pact, the warriors could safely unleash the ferocity and the rawness of their emotions. The heroes then went home to their families and duties, head held high. It was an implicit covenant not to discuss or recount the horrors they endured or inflicted during battles. They were expected to be ardent and powerful protectors of their dominions and of the monarchies that ruled them.

The music faded and the lap dancer gently tried

to disengage herself from Gabriel's tight embrace. He snapped out of his reverie as he jerked up his head from the fragrance of her bosom. Gabriel felt dizzy and disoriented to be so abruptly catapulted back into his body in current time and space. The woman showed concern and caring in her eyes, but whispered to him that the dance was over. Gabriel beheld her exquisite face that looked so much like his temple lover. He was confused and emotional from his journey back in time; he held on to her and begged her to spend the night with him. She softly but firmly said that her body was not for sale; her job was only to dance. Embarrassed, Gabriel apologized and stumbled out of the room to look for Chris, trying to shake off the fuzzy influence of pot and the surreal dream that he just stepped out of. He had never gone to a prostitute before and he was afraid that he might have offended the lap dancer. During the twenty-some years of his traveling career, he had always prided himself in not engaging with the seamy side of life, though he occasionally allowed himself to indulge in casual romance. Generally he was full of respect for women.

On the way home, Chris inquired whether Gabriel had a good time, while touting his own. Gabriel wanted to tell him what a magnificent performer the dancer was, but his head was all mixed-up. He thought, 'was it this woman or was it my temple lover that I saw dancing tonight?' He had never experienced a dream or a past life scenario so vividly before, though he believed in the possibility of reincarnation. He was baffled and he tried to convince himself that the encounter was all a hallucination. He was hoping that the cold air of the San Francisco night would clear his confusion, but everything remained a blur. He muttered a "thank you" to Chris when they got to his apartment. Gabriel just wanted to go to bed; he had a splitting headache. He was still disturbed by his indecent proposal to the lap dancer.

Gabriel had a fitful night, tossing and turning through waves of turbulent dreams. He was back at the temple courtyard, this time returning from another battle. He looked eagerly for his sweetheart everywhere but there was no trace of her. He frantically inquired with the dancers, musicians and attendants. No one seemed to have seen her for a long time, yet he detected fear and secrecy in their eyes. He knew they were not telling him the whole truth, but he failed to pry any more information out of them. He implored the goddess statues, but they only looked back at him with compassion in their smiles that were sculpted in stone. In the dream he had lost her forever. An overwhelming despair befell him. He never returned to that temple again.

Despite the grandeur, honors, titles and wealth bestowed upon him for his valiant conquests, he ironically died an old man with a secretly broken heart for he had lost the love of his life. His inner light had been extinguished with her mysterious vanishing. Though a loving family and friends who revered him surrounded him with care, his temple dancer was the only holy vessel to whom he had bequeathed his sacred fire. No other lovers were able to touch his core as she had.

Gabriel woke up the next day and felt dried-up tears on his face. He was quite shaken up by the surreal events of the night before, which left a deep impact in his heart. Though he had always been an open-minded renaissance man—having witnessed many amazing and bizarre situations around the world during his assignments—he had never felt such intense emotions before. In fact, he had never experienced this kind of deep sorrow, even after breaking up with his previously significant others. None of the wonderful women he had been with could arouse the kind of intensity that was just revealed to him so miraculously. Now in his mid-forties, he was content to be teased by friends as a confirmed bachelor. He had taken a relaxed stance toward relationships, for in his heart he never felt committed in the way he did in his dream. He realized now that pretty faces, even with good hearts and intentions, could not fulfill his forlorn yearning.

Gabriel felt restless and he walked out to Grant Avenue for some fresh morning air. As he distractedly sauntered by a bakery, he collided into a woman who was coming out the door with a baguette in her hand. He profusely apologized and was shocked to notice that she was the dancer from the club last night, though she didn't have any make-up on her face and she wore a casual beige sweater and jeans—a far cry from the dazzles of her costumed persona. She looked lovely to him; he would recognize those piercing eyes anywhere. His heart stopped and he was speechless. She remembered him too and looked a bit embarrassed and vulnerable. Gabriel recovered quickly and inquired whether she lived nearby. She nodded imperceptibly. To break the ice, he stuck out a hand and introduced himself for the first time. She responded with a friendly smile, saying that her name was Sabrina. He desperately did not want to lose sight of her; this coincidence was too uncanny. He thought quickly on his feet; and awkwardly invited her to join him for coffee or breakfast at the corner café. She hesitated for a moment but then graciously accepted.

Over latte and pastries, Gabriel solemnly apologized for his behavior of the previous night and sheepishly admitted to her that he had never experienced a lap dance before. Sabrina chuckled and teasingly said that she might not have done a good job, since he left so abruptly. Gabriel was now truly mortified and confessed that he had a very confusing night. He openly shared with her that he had lapsed into some kind of time warp and that he had journeyed into a surreal situation that astounded him. A comprehension dawned on her face and she commented that indeed he seemed to be in a different world while she was dancing, that he didn't appear to be focusing on her at all. She shyly and curiously asked what had transpired for him. She looked so innocent and so warm his heart just melted under her gaze. "Do you believe in past lives?" he asked tentatively.

"Yes, I think so, though I haven't explored any of my own," she said with anticipated interest. Gabriel somehow felt comfortable telling her about the experience he had in the bar and he also told her about his subsequent dream, swearing to her that this was not a come-on. His stories brought tears to her eyes. Gabriel noticed with delight that he had touched her sensitive soul. Sabrina asked what time period his experience was in; he thought it might have been in ancient Persia or some other olden country. She remarked that she had an affinity for all things Persian—from poetry, philosophy, and dance, to spiritual mysteries. That explained to him her choice of garments last night.

Gabrial delicately probed her as to why she had chosen a lap dancing profession. Sabrina replied that she was in a full-time master's program at the Institute of Transpersonal Psychology, which didn't leave her much time to work. Since she was trained in various forms of dancing, she enjoyed this new part-time job as a lap dancer. She made a lot of fast money with tips, which afforded her a good way to support herself. She tried to look brave and casual, saying that such a job gave her the freedom to devote herself to studying and taking courses during the daytime. Gabriel did not comment;

it was not his place to judge her choices in any way. He then shared about himself and some vignettes of his career in photography. Hours flew by and they fell into a natural ease talking to each other. Gabriel expectantly asked whether he could see her again. She noticed his attraction toward her and she seemed to enjoy his company also, but she made it clear that she welcomed friendship only, nothing more.

In the following days and weeks, Gabriel was relieved that he wasn't obliged to go on any out-of-town or overseas assignments, so he could have the luxury of spending time with Sabrina. They met for coffee, hung out at each other's places, and got to know each other better, but Sabrina steered clear of getting intimate with him. Gabriel was already falling hard for her; his heart ached with longing each time he beheld her delicate beauty. He confided in Chris but Chris warned him to be careful and not to give of himself to women who earned money with their seduction. However, Gabriel could not get her out of his mind; everything about her felt so familiar to him. Her presence triggered a powerful response in his heart, as though she was his temple dancer come alive. The two realities were now merged into one. He saw transposed on her face his ancient lover's features. The manners of her "past-self" were tangible to him. Just like the warrior who confessed to his lover, Gabriel instinctively felt he could trust her and tell her anything. She always showed interest and seemed to appreciate his points of view about life and she was fascinated by his travel stories. She seemed at least a good ten years younger than him, but she possessed a quiet wisdom beyond her years, as she frequently made thoughtful remarks.

He knew it was crazy to be in love with an erotic dancer who didn't want him, but he craved her company and endlessly fantasized about making love to her. He made any excuse to see her, enticing her with his home-cooked dinners, or inviting her out for a stroll whenever he could pry her away from her studies. Though she was careful in not giving him any signal of sexual interest, she was tender and caring in listening to him share about his life, and she adored his artistic work. Gabriel dreamed of photographing her one day in her sensual poses.

Sabrina finally opened up and shared more about her life and her dream to become a healer for women. That was why she gave up a middle-management career at a hospital to pursue her graduate degree. She revealed that she was emotionally abused as a child. Her father was chauvinistic and a controlling alcoholic; this left her deeply scarred. Her mother seemed to be unable to protect herself and her child; she played the role of resigned subservience. Sabrina was well aware that her dream to heal others was ultimately a desire to heal herself.

She gradually divulged more about her views on her job. She admitted she enjoyed feeling a certain kind of power over men in her work environment. She had certainly met the full spectrum of the male species, from the boastful and the vulgar, to the pathetic and the lonely as well as men who, deep down, felt helpless with women. She told him that there was a peculiar balance of power in the world of erotic dancing. It was the unattainable elusiveness of luscious dreams that kept men yearning for more and kept them coming back. While the dancers seemed to put themselves in vulnerable situations, they had a certain authority to keep men at bay in a high-end bar, such as the one she worked at. The dancers were protected by their work protocols and their brawny managers, who kept a watchful eye against any offensively lewd behavior from patrons. Gabriel challenged her that such a view held an inherent hostility toward men and contempt toward them. Sabrina didn't totally deny it; she acknowledged that she felt a subconscious anger toward this male-dominated world from a very young age; it went beyond her unhappy childhood. "Maybe it's a dormant memory of rage from being victimized by patriarchal tyranny, which might have stemmed from circumstances in other lifetimes," she wondered out loud.

Gabriel was quite troubled by Sabrina's lopsided view of power. He felt she went about her unconscious revenge on men in the wrong direction. He reflected many times about the warrior lifetime that was revealed to him and which still affected him emotionally. He sensed that his life was somehow inextricably linked to Sabrina's across time and space, connected by the ancient echoes of their deep love. Even her personality and her temperaments were familiar to him, evoking memories of how he and his temple maiden loved each other with innocent abandon. Her scent was like a magnet to him, eliciting feelings that were deeply buried until recently. It was as though he was now living two parallel lives where interchangeable passages were superimposed upon each other. However, the incongruity of a temple dancer offering sacred ecstasy and a lap dancer selling hopes of dreams did not elude him. The situation was ironic; he traveled the world photographing splendors and visions, only to finally find his ancient love in his own neighborhood in the role of an exotic dancer. His whole life up to now was about moving forward. Little did he know he needed to gaze backward into an unrequited love in order to discover his own true heart.

Gabriel gradually felt a certain protectiveness toward Sabrina, beyond mere nostalgia of an elusive past. He wanted to help her find the right path to heal her wounds, even if she might never want him to be her lover. This was the first time he loved beyond just selfish wanting. Maybe there was a seed of the fearless and noble warrior still in him, with impeccable self-discipline and the strength of mind to control his own emotional needs. He now felt his sense of duty in life was to some greater meaning other than himself. Being in love with Sabrina—without her reciprocation—had somehow matured him into a better man. He felt a deep caring for her. He liked the purity of his own heart when he encouraged her, without any ulterior motive on his part, to pursue healing of her psychological wounds.

With the warrior's honor fused into the lover in him,

he felt compassion and a sense of connectedness with her humanity and her frailty. Nonetheless, he honestly believed that using manipulation to fight manipulation, no matter how subtle, could never bring about a better world. This conviction of his was strengthened by the myriad encounters he had as a worldwide photographer. He had witnessed lives in ruin one too many times under shady circumstances. He cautioned Sabrina that she might be playing with fire by feeding the dark dreams of male egos. She was defiant to him but she privately felt blessed to be loved by someone with such a noble heart, and her stance gradually softened. She agreed to reflect on the deeper aspects of her core wounds. Several days later she told him that she was going away for three weeks on a school retreat for intensive training in hypnotherapy, and wouldn't be able to be reached by phone. Gabriel knew he would miss her terribly.

A few weeks passed. It was another late Saturday evening and Gabriel had just come home from an assignment in Idaho. There was an urgent knock on his door and he expected to see his friend Chris with a six-pack of beer in hand. To his delighted surprise, it was Sabrina, standing there looking vulnerable and fragile.

She threw herself passionately into his arms and he embraced her with joy, thrilled by this sudden pleasure. They kissed for the first time, without restraint. She smelled and tasted like heaven to him, arousing in him fierce love and protectiveness. Gabriel was elated and tried to question her with his eyes, but she put a finger on his lips, searched his eyes for resonance, and bashfully led him toward his bedroom. He lay on the bed as she sat on top of him and slowly shed her layers of clothing. He went wild with desire and his heart pounded hard, drumming out all the suppressed longings of the last few months. Sabrina was now swaying rhythmically to an internal melody; her half-covered figure was utterly captivating.

In the dim room, her shapely feminine silhouette was like a coiled serpent rising up seductively, with her hands dancing in sensuous mudra-like gestures. His temple dancer had once again come alive! She gracefully bared her breasts and lowered herself onto his mouth to let him taste her taut jewels. He was in bliss holding her dainty waist while reveling in her and hungrily nibbling on her velvety skin. He relished the excitement of seeing her breasts released from the confining bras, looking rounder and more luscious than the first time he saw her in her dancing garb. He took her in his arms and savored her scent, caressing her hair, kissing her belly button and licking the crevices in between her beautifully shaped toes, which drove him even wilder with desire. These were the same dancing feet eons ago that had given the warrior so much pleasure. He kissed her avidly, tasting her tongue and drinking in her elixir. She whispered softly in his ears, with him inhaling each of her breath. Sabrina felt utterly cherished. When Gabriel became so hard he could barely stand it, she slid down, using her tongue to make swirls around his crown, as her hand clasped his shaft and stroked him in tantalizing ways that inflamed him even more.

She was now uninhibited, in ecstatic passion and hot blushes from the excited state, as though they had always made love to each other. When Gabriel came close to exploding, she slowed down and lovingly guided his rhythm inside of her. He then took over and made love to her with unrestrained torrid thrusts, which sparked moans of euphoric delight from her. They basked in a joyfully orgasmic fire together, sending a tsunami of sensation throughout their bodies. They looked adoringly into each other's eyes and their hearts coalesced into a vortex of exultation. Every fiber in Gabriel's being recognized who she was. At long last, his beloved had come home. As they relaxed into a tender embrace, Sabrina related her story for the first time, quivering with emotion.

During her hypnotherapy training and practice sessions, Sabrina had learned to relax into an egoless state and let go of her defenses. She was able to delve deeply into the recesses of her psyche, revealing the cause of her stubborn rage toward men. This unconscious fury that constrained her from loving fully had influenced her in the past to make painful relationship choices in her life. Her soul opened up to re-experience the life of the temple dancer. Her own discovery paralleled Gabriel's past life recount. At first her conscious mind still struggled with the remembrance, but too many visions and images flooded her memory in the hypnotic state, beyond the reach of her thinking mind. She was like an observer watching movie scenes unreeling in front of her, an experience beyond imagination. She was undeniably the beloved temple dancer of a warrior in that life. She had honed her devotional dance of passion for the Goddess to such exquisite perfection that she was chosen by the high-ranking priests to be a sacrificial offering to the

Gods. She was aware of the jealousy of the priests, which perplexed her and made her uncomfortable. They seemed to be envious of her fervent piety to the Goddess. She remembered vividly how the impassive executioner slit her throat with precision in a dark night's ceremony, while priestesses danced ecstatically and chanted to welcome the almighty Gods to feast on her blood. Her shattering scream of pain and terror was interpreted as a cry of ecstasy in veneration to the deities. She was bewildered and in her dying breath she wondered why being devoted to the Goddess of Love would cost her the precious life she cherished.

Gabriel was earnestly grieving with her as Sabrina shared her experience of the story. Strong sentiments overcame him as he was reliving his feelings of that lifetime. His whole body trembled with outrage toward those barbaric times of ancient pagan rites. He now understood why he—the warrior in the dream—sensed fear in some of the dancers' eyes when he inquired of his lover's whereabouts.

As they were drying each other's tears, Gabriel tenderly caressed Sabrina, intuiting that her emotions were still fragile from recalling the traumatic experience. As her shivering started to ebb, Sabrina vulnerably confessed that she had felt a great kinship toward him since the first time she met him. The dance she did for him that night was propelled and inspired by a fire in her heart. The fact that Gabriel seemed to be somewhere else during her dance had actually freed her to perform even more passionately without restraint. When he revealed his attraction to her in subsequent days, she felt she couldn't respond because she had vowed to never invite clients into her heart. Her job symbolized for her a subconscious revenge on men who had subjugated her. Sabrina now realized that her obsessive rage was an excuse to keep her from manifesting her true feminine strength and integrity. She quit her job the day she came home from the retreat and now her heart felt free to love. She expressed her deep gratitude to Gabriel for being the catalyst to help her unlock her inexplicable wound. Their tears had washed away the constriction in both of their hearts.

They were now together once again, feeling sublime as they cherished each other in body, mind and soul. It dawned on them that the spirit lived forever. Gabriel ruminated, as another layer of understanding awakened in him, 'Each life is only a passage of growth impelling the next evolution of consciousness, transmuting painful karmic experiences into positive dharma when love prevails.' Their souls' devotion to each other had pulled them through eons to reunite at this moment. Here they were, alive and well, after an eternity of separation. They realized that ultimately love and forgiveness was the eternal flame, beyond the veils of time and space, beyond the limitations of any lifetime.

A Destined Rendezvous

Starseeds reunited, acknowledging their shared essence.
They join with open eyes and hearts
in dimensions beyond the finite.

A Destined Rendezvous

Naxi Tribe in Lijiang, China, Year 261 BCE

MALU was a young woman of the Mosuo community, which was one of the Naxi ethnic clans, living in a picturesque rural area outside of Lijiang, on the shores of the graceful Lugu Lake. Lijiang was an ancient city, idyllically nestled in the valley of the sacred Jade Dragon Snow Mountain, amidst other mighty ranges of Northwestern Yunnan Province. Her people was one of the primordial indigenous tribes, dating back at least a thousand years prior to recorded history, to even before this region was known as China.

The Naxi were descendants of an ancient nomadic tribe that had long ago given up their wandering and settled in this beautiful basin where they lived in harmony with their surroundings. Their closeness to the land made them natural farmers—generally making a living by tending to crops and herding yaks. Their peaceful rhythm with nature was not learned, it was their breath of everyday life. The Naxi also loved planting trees and flowers as a regular ritual, understanding humanity's participation in the mysteries of the land's regenerative magic. They adored the blossoms of plum trees, the cheerful chrysanthemums and the multitude of exquisite orchids.

The Naxi tribe was a matrilineal society with a respect for patrilineal contributions. They held a prehistoric family system with a unique polytheistic marital convention. They regarded females as the roots and trunks that stabilized their community, and males as branches and leaves that expressed their skills and arts to enliven the vitality of their society. The Mosuo people did not have a monogamous marriage structure of husband and wife. Instead they practiced a peculiar custom of union called *Axia*—meaning *lover*—in which a man and a woman did not establish a family. When night fell, a man would go to a woman's house or to her private *love cave*, and then he would leave before dawn. It was a unique arrangement of "walk-in" marriage that worked well in their tradition. Whenever a woman fancied a man to whom she felt attracted, she would be the one who took the initiative to invite him into her life but he would never live with her. A woman's family was exclusively for matrilineal members. When boys were born, uncles on the mother's side of the family—who served as male models or surrogate fathers—looked after them and eventually taught the young men skills such as construction, carpentry and sculpting. Women in the household largely tended to the girls; and they made most of the livelihood decisions by committee for the welfare of the entire village.

Malu lived with her grandmother, mother, two aunts, her younger sister and two of her mother's brothers. Men were allowed in the household as long as they were blood relations of the females in the family. Women then, naturally, were the most highly respected. They managed the family system and their community. Men were their right-hand help and they were not belittled. The Mosuo tribe lived in harmony with one another. They were the walking Yin and Yang of nature that they revered. Since the Naxi people believed in the magic of flowers, they had a special tradition to *read* and *evaluate* flowers in meticulous processes.

Malu was well versed in flower meditation and in spiritual appraisal of the blossoms. She held the honored position of a young shamaness and she didn't need to tend to farm chores. Her grandmother Solua had been grooming her since childhood for upholding this subtle yet powerful lineage of shamanism that spanned generations in her family. Solua herself was the current matriarch shamaness and medicine woman of the village.

The Mosuo's love of the land afforded them a deep mystical alignment with humanity's spiritual origin and the intelligence of the unseen world. Whenever flowers were in full bloom, Solua loved to invite relatives and friends to come and surround Malu who would then *read* the messages that the flowers held for them. She would go into a trance, transmitting prophetic poems from the flower kingdom to guide their upcoming years.

Because of her distinguished position, Malu's clothing was exquisitely tended to with extra fine trims on her gown, black jacket and flowing long sleeves. Her pleated skirt was adorned with motifs of delicate flowers. She wore a tastefully embroidered sheepskin cape with colorful images of the Sun, stars and otherworldly beings, finished with dangling beaded tassels. Her shiny black hair was braided in long tresses, woven with elaborate beadwork and lingering strands of dark blue silk threads, which hung down her waist. She simply was a vision of loveliness.

Yet Malu did not give in to affectation; she felt at home in her attires and with her mission. She was now in her mid twenties with the luscious experience of a fully bloomed woman. The art of sexual pleasures had been part of her natural training since her teenage years.

She had been choosing lovers with ease and delight. Whenever she had time, Malu enjoyed carving erotic figures with spiritual meanings into the walls of her *love cave*—a real grotto that she adorned with cozy cushioning and colorful fabrics, hidden from view of her family dwelling. She had an implicit pact with the fireflies to fill her love nest with scintillating light during amorous encounters with her lovers. She was potent in her full sexual maturity; she was Earth Goddess come alive in a woman's body.

There was one particular handsome fellow named Gebao whom Malu favored the most. She was always seized by an intoxication that abounded with freedom and abandon whenever they were together. She became his devoted lover and even pledged a long-term connection to him. Gebao was a gifted sculptor, an accomplished musician and a prominent entertainer in the village ceremonies for rain and for the virility of the tribesmen. He was the finest dancer of their pictograph DongBa language, which could be expressed through movements, speech or writing. When Malu watched him perform in a festival for the first time, he touched her heart like no other.

Malu was his *Song of the Night*. She weaved gossamer

magic of love and dowsed him with enchantment. When he gazed into the exquisiteness reflected in her intense eyes, he wanted to dwell in her dreams forever and reside in her heart. He was inebriated from her embrace and never wanted to surface again. With her, he was a roaring fire with wild wanting. She brought joy, laughter and ecstasy into his life. She fanned the cauldron of his very essence with voluptuous and encompassing love. In moments of erotic bliss between them, he felt her surrender to his vigorous masculinity— her pulsating heart beating the same rhythm as his.

His inflamed rod loved to thrust deeply into her throbbing sea of pleasure. They endlessly discovered new horizons of sensuous elation through their lovemaking. He felt his burning candle erupting into floods of light every time he climaxed with her. Being in love with Malu, Gebao was inspired to manifest the best of his strength. His sexuality united his spirituality and his creative forces, permeating everything that he did. His artistic work culminated to its finest.

Gebao was, however, a man of exceptionally strong character and he was discontented with their clan's matriarchal system, which did not choose committed unions. He wanted Malu to be his one and only woman but her belief was so well entrenched in her matrilineal upbringing that she didn't know how to empathize with his yearning. She loved him dearly and was loyal to him in her own way; she saw no need to change the Mosuo traditions.

Gebao had gone into Lijiang many times to sell his sculptures; he had observed the monogamous marital system of the Chinese people who lived there. He so envied the stability of their homemaking, with laughter of children playing in the courtyards. How he desired to taste family life with Malu! After many frustrated attempts to convince her to elope and to marry him, he left one day without a trace, and he had not returned since. Rumors circulated around that he had joined the warlords who were ruling the Lijiang vicinities at the time and that he had become a fierce commander of war himself.

Malu could have never predicted that his absence would hit her so hard. She went into fits of tears and longing. She felt angry of being betrayed, although she knew she was the one who rejected his aching for something more. She had sunk into a stupor of loss. His tenderness was forever etched in her heart and she realized too late of her abiding love for him. She became depressed and despondent, though she tried hard to hide it from others. Her culture did not understand weakness toward an *Axia*. Even her flower evaluations suffered; she couldn't quite concentrate to *read* them with focused accuracy. She made excuses to be alone so she could reflect on her regrets, and silently ask for his forgiveness. They were now forever separated by an irreversible chasm. Her inner core was as desolate as the barren land in winter. She had no interest to entice any other *Axia* into her *love cave*. Her life now was broken pieces of shattered dreams. She missed him more than she could endure.

Nothing escaped the sharp eyes of her grandmother Solua. One day she came to bait Malu out of her *cave* where she usually hid herself these days. Malu could no longer sustain a stoic appearance in her comforting embrace, the floodgate of tears broke and the deluge of grief surged forward. Solua felt that it was time to tell her granddaughter the greater truth behind her love story with Gebao—that he wasn't just another *Axia*. She started by reminding Malu that the Naxi people came from the stars and that their tribe had a pre-destined mission in contribution to the future evolution of humanity. It was their sacred duty to live the unbroken lineage of this benign matrilineal practice, side by side with the dominant patriarchal system through the ages, until the time came for a new flourishing of equal partnership between the sexes.

Malu and Gebao were preordained *Starseeded lovers* to experience intense love of equals, in spite of the Naxi practices. Their souls were to remember this love in future reincarnations to sustain them through trials and errors of the human condition, under strenuous tests of male-controlled societies that subjugated women, overtly or subtly, in which females survived by submission, manipulations or through various disguises of deceit. However, women would revolutionize the collective structures one day, which would announce the pre-dawning of a more equal society. Matriarchy and patriarchy would take turns being the dominant belief system through the ages. Such was the cosmic agreement to balance the light and the dark of duality in three-dimensional existence, until such a time that human evolution could come to a new equilibrium.

Life in a body was a sacred experiment of the *Starseeded Spirits* who came to experience themselves as *Matter* on this beautiful planet. Earth has a mysterious *consciousness* that could hold resonance for both spirit and matter. Both human sexes—representing the polarization of Yin and Yang—would taste life at its best through love, and at its worst through conflicts and mutual abuses.

By choice and remembrance, humanity would one day return to the *Light* of Spirit—symbolized by the radiance of the Sun, and to the *Love* that fueled Spirit—embodied by the abundant Earth. The gift of their Mosuo way would serve humanity in exemplifying the *all-encompassing* love of Ancient Mother—the God-source of all regenerative creations, unencumbered by male-dictated laws. Lugu Lake, the shores on which they would live for millenia, is one of the most magical bodies of waters in the world that holds the energetic echo of the Divine Mother force. Pristine Lugu stores some heightened frequencies of sunlight, fused with the crystalline core of Earth, which purify souls. Some day this lake would play a part to help humankind remember the cosmic drama of the intended experiment of *Matter* returning to *Light*.

Solua explained why the Naxi culture was one of the chosen tribes to carry out this sacred engagement. It had a lot to do with the tribe's location of settlement. Lijiang, situated between Yunnan and Tibet, was a tea and horse-trading route, and also a natural port in the Southern Silk Road. Its people easily absorbed myriad civilizations of many other nationalities. Besides, the current warring states dominating their region brought in foreign cultural practices that integrated many religious belief systems—Taoism which was the most ancient philosophical foundation of China, Tibetan Buddhism of the nearby Central Plain, and the Naxi's own shamanism, which espoused a multitude of spiritual traditions. They were a Mother Nature-based people who could coexist with and assimilate all in harmony. This condition made it natural for their indigenous culture to merge with the world but retain their resilient and independent spirit of purity. For centuries to come they would serve humanity's evolution in many ways with their quiet wisdom of peace.

Malu's personal tragedy in this lifetime was her spirit's divine pact with Gebao for him to explore his dark night of the soul. All men, in one incarnation or another, were meant to experience the horrors of war so they would recall, deep in their bones, the pointless cruelty of men's violence toward one another through the ages. They would eventually rise together with their beloveds to eradicate this atrocity from existence. Men held the key to unlock the psychic jail in which they imprisoned one another. Gebao would stand strong and clear for peace one day, in some future life.

Malu and Gebao would encounter each other in many lives to come, playing different roles for each other, to be the catalysts of reminding the other for learning true compassion through the sufferings they each would confront again and again. They represented a *love before time*—ancient Father Sky and Mother Earth energies at the source of creation, at the cradle of light undivided—equal partners in all ways.

Starseeds formed an unmistakable forcefield of light, radiating the purest essence of unconditional love. It was necessary for Malu to have lived a matrilineal heritage, and for Gebao to experience patriarchy in its full spectrum. Eventually neither legacy would last because they both represented imbalance, even though some of the traditions and guiding principles in each of the constructs might have been beneficial. Solua predicted that the new Golden Age of Unity would arrive after the cycles of duality took their turns to express all the various aspects of the light and dark of lopsided powers between the sexes. Unity consciousness would prevail, because each human being came to life as a unit of undivided light.

Solua continued to foretell that every time Malu and Gebao reunite, the alignment of their magnetized momentums would build upon each other. When Spirit descends and Earth ascends to fuse the frequency, a state of merging is formed. It clicks into coalescence, as two pieces of a puzzle fitting perfectly, regardless of the roles their souls would choose to play. They would learn to be compassionate in knowing that they might not be together in idealistic union in each lifetime. It would be essential for them to hold their hearts pure and whole, in order to alchemize love to its finest. They would be reborn again and again as the eternal images of their spiritual identities. To reach the summit of an enlightened love would not be possible until they kept shedding old binary patterning of lifetimes, thus cleansing their souls, as an artist would polish a precious piece of jade to reveal its lushest shine.

"When the Golden Solar Age age comes due in which humans would be ripe for true partnership," said Solua, "you need to be whole in yourself, in ecstatic unconditional love. Only then can you inaugurate the soul of Gebao into his new *kingship*. You will initiate him into the core purpose of his life and awaken his consciousness to the new height of holding a cosmic responsibility and wisdom for humanity. He will become an emblem of the Sun, reaching for its zenith. It is then that Solar brilliance and Earth's nectar fuse into one magnificent unity; all illusions of separateness will evaporate like a mist."

Solua patiently shared her knowledge with confidence, braiding Malu's tresses: "The higher purpose of love is the orgasmic pinnacle of body, mind and soul, moving euphorically closer to the original breath of life that emanates from everywhere in the cosmos. When you unite as one in this heightened state, you are two parts of a key that fit back together to realize the destined dance of creation. *Starseeds* are like a hologram—a small fragment that contains the entire reflection of the Universe."

Malu asked when the Enlightened Age would arrive in which she could reunite with Gebao in blissful love. "It might not be until another two thousand years. Meanwhile you can only keep purifying your own soul's development through rebirths," answered Solua compassionately. She added that although she was clairvoyant, she couldn't help speed up the process of the Universe. The evolution of humanity on this planet has its own pre-destined unfolding; cosmic timing has its omniscient wisdom.

Malu cultivated her calm acceptance of being part of a higher purpose. She transmuted her suffering into boundless love for her tribe, untiringly giving of herself to the community. She grew to be wiser and more self-assured with a deep-seated knowing of her covenant. She became a most compassionate shamaness of her time.

Lijiang, China, Year 2011 CE

MALINA breathes in the pristine air and exhales her first puff of freshness in the cool April morning. She has been in Lijiang for a few days now. She loves welcoming the morning air when she gets up, looking out the window into the quaint Chinese courtyard of the old-fashioned inn where she stays, in the heart of town. She has yet to experience air quality this clean anywhere else in China. Her heart opens wide with joy, relishing the magnificence of this ancient city—a World Heritage Site that is cuddled in the bosom of dramatic snow-capped mountains between the highland plateaus of Yunnan and Tibet.

She appreciates that Lijiang is not a place given

to posturing. This city has confidently retained a historic landscape of authenticity where cars are off-limit. She loves its unique architecture for the blending of elements from several exotic cultures, which had merged over many centuries. With hundreds of old bridges crisscrossing through town, this stunning panorama possesses an antiquated water-supply system of great ingenuity that still functions effectively today. The river running into the city includes a network of meandering canals that flow abundantly along the glistening cobblestoned streets. Almost every dwelling—tile-roofed structures of soil, wood and stone, adorned by windows carved with flowers, birds and animals—is surrounded by streams and swaying willows.

Lijiang offers a rare glimpse into the lives of China's many distinctive indigenous minorities—the Naxi tribe being the main ethnic culture—which have been flourishing for thousands of years in this region. The Naxi women today are still dressed in their ancient-style blue blouses and pants, wrapped with a black apron, roaming the streets with heavy baskets filled with produce on their backs, or a baby tucked away in a brightly colored cloth securely cinched to the waist. They are short but stout, going about their busy days with purposeful expressions on their sun-drenched faces. The men, generally sporting the traditional cowboy-like Naxi hats, wear more varied clothing, blending ethnic with modern casual attire. Malina notices, with a chuckle, how they either lounge on benches, chatting with one another or they nonchalantly accompany their click-clacking animal friends on the cobblestones. It is obvious to her that their matriarchal custom is still alive and well.

Malina has been anticipating the exploration of this fascinating culture for a while now. She owns a jewelry business specializing in indigenous beadwork. She has traveled to many places in the world and loves her wonderful encounters with aboriginal tribes. Her career has reached a point where she can take more time off, leaving the business in the capable hands of a reliable management team. Malina plans to stay in Yunnan for a month to leisurely investigate into the mysteries of this region, and of its many minorities. She has researched quite a bit about the Naxi people and their DongBa legacy—the written hieroglyphs and records of their culture and philosophy—which is more ancient than even the Chinese civilization. She heard that the DongBa shamans are well versed in medicine, literature, alchemy and arts; Malina looks forward to having first-hand experience of their magic. Everything she has read somehow feels eerily familiar to her.

Her exposure to tribal cultures, spanning many years, has naturally groomed Malina to become very attuned to spiritual aspects of life. She was mentored by Native-American elders on forgiveness, guided by Peruvian shamans to unravel the dark reaches of her psyche, healed of nagging psycho-spiritual wounds by Celtic Druids, taught by Chinese Taoist sages who inspired in her a reverential love for the mystical powers of nature. She felt very blessed to have partaken entheogens of various ethnic communities. Those sacred medicines had contributed to her inner growth by leaps and bounds, pushing her light-years ahead of any conventional talk-therapies.

Though the twists and turns of her life seemed to have presented insurmountable challenges and pains through the years, she presently feels liberated and whole within herself. Though she is still single and would love to have a life partner with whom to share experiences, she doesn't feel any urge or anxiety about relationships anymore. Malina had gone through too much heartbreak to foolishly jump into any romance.

She would be at peace with remaining alone in this lifetime if that were her fate. She is a person of high ideals and with deep perspectives about life. Over the years, it has been challenging for her to meet someone who could truly resonate with her inner self. Men in her life had wanted her for themselves in conventional and selfish ways of possessiveness. She, on the other hand, has always known that her destiny is in service to a greater whole, and not in self-absorbed cocooning. She yearns for a partner who feels similarly in order to grow together and to commit in serving a brighter future for all.

Malina has no bitterness or regrets about her experiences in life, no matter how much she had suffered, especially in relationships with men. She was married once briefly many years ago and has no illusions about this convention either. She has an inner understanding that her soul's development has culminated into a certain stage of acuity. She seems to have pledged to incarnate in this life to complete negative karma with people who had been important to her soul in previous lifetimes. Though some of the circumstances were so excruciating that they almost caused a nervous breakdown, she doesn't hold any more resentment. Malina has released herself even from forgiveness, knowing deep inside that there is ultimately nothing to forgive. Her soul is a co-creator with the God-consciousness to live through every situation for her own soul's evolution. At age 45, Malina feels happy and excited at long last about fully living every moment. She senses a new chapter of her life is just beginning. She feels younger and less burdened emotionally than ever before. Malina has an innately deep love for people and the world seems to respond to her with open arms. She appreciates spending time working on meaningful causes to ease the plight of indigenous tribes in different parts of the world.

She has recently come across the Mayan Calendar and its prophesy of the impending Golden Solar Age, which gives her true hope for the future of humanity. Though the complex mathematical calculations of the Calendar elude her, Malina instinctively resonates with its profound wisdom. The Mayan's enlightened knowledge explains time in mystical dimensions of human evolution with evident tracking of sweeping historical changes in the world through the millennia. She has been acutely aware that her own life events flow along the waves of this cosmic time. She has been pondering her next role of contribution to Unity Consciousness and Malina is curious as to how it will unfold. That is the matter of the ego mind, constantly wanting to know, and yet so many times life leads her through winding roads that surprise her.

With sharpened psychic abilities through years of practice, she intuits that something is still missing for her to fully blossom into her soul's mission. She inherently knows that there's something awaiting her on the Eastern shores. She is a Chinese-American and yet she has not had the opportunity to immerse herself in Chinese mysticism. Though she has traveled to China many times in search of that elusive something, she has not been able to stumble upon it. China is much more open nowadays to religions of various beliefs, but spiritualism in its pure form seems too intangible to reach, especially amidst the technological frenzy of current times. She has lived through supernatural manifestations of various disciplines, but she has yet to experience transcendental secrets from the East, which remain elusive to the world outside of gurus' teachings, religious practices such as Tibetan Buddhism, or miracles performed by ascetic Sadhus in India.

One day not long ago, when Malina awoke and

basked in the sweet fragrance of honeysuckles outside her bedroom window, she heard a flower deva whisper to her: " it's time to go to Lijiang." She took it as a matter of fact with joyous curiosity and started making her plans for the journey—she somehow felt the *Eastern Promise* was close to unveiling itself. Over the years, Malina has been accustomed to Spirit's calls, which usually turned out to be accurate and revealing. She no longer questions these cryptic invitations; she has coined them *cosmic crumbs* and usually follows them, though with trepidation at times.

On the flight from New York to China, an elegant elderly woman sat next to Malina and kept smiling gently at her, revealing a deep knowing through her eyes. There was a vibration of empathy between them. Malina sensed that this woman embodied a timeless wisdom of the universal grandmother. They chatted genially with each other. When they arrived in Beijing, Malina said goodbye to her with affection, before heading off to her plane transfer to Lijiang. The woman wished Malina a safe journey and enigmatically murmured: "You'll meet your destiny there. Cherish it!" Then she disappeared amongst the thousands of hurried travelers at the busy airport.

Malina just now recalls this serendipitous encounter as she meanders through the narrow streets and alleys—filled with dizzying displays of souvenirs, tribal embroidered apparels, Naxi sculptures and carvings that look too commercial and too bright in color for her taste. There are overflowing ethnic silver jewelries and unending selections of scarves made of hemp and silk. She is delighted to find, on long strands of necklaces or tasseled ornaments, some very unusual beadwork consisted of a variety of dried nuts and miniscule dried gourds that she has never seen before. Her mind is not on business though, so she just files away the business cards she picks up from the artisans so she can follow-up some other day.

What stops Malina suddenly in her tracks is a small Naxi artisan shop tucked between two larger handicraft stores. The wood sculptures inside are the most refined yet that she has seen. Naxi art is filled with spiritual tales of the Sun, Moon and stars. It also abounds with legends of flower deities, talking animals and star people in bursts of colors, geometric designs, and in mind-altering waves and patterns crisscrossing through. Almost every piece of art in the shop is exquisitely rendered, esthetically displayed to tell the stories. The colors are much more subdued than the thousands that she has seen in other shops and galleries, and the portrayals have a modern twist to them. Malina' eyes are drawn to two small sculptures, each about a square foot, that make her catch her breath for some reason. Tears fill her eyes inexplicably.

One is a rendition of a woman's visage prominently engraved at the forefront of the sculpture, facing a man's profile depicted in a half moon. Her eyes are with yearning, but his face looks sad. The other woodcarving illustrates a man's and a woman's profiles flowing toward each other, with lotuses coming out of them and psychedelic swirls entwining them. Malina asks the storekeeper for the prices, which are so reasonable that she doesn't hesitate to buy them on the spot. The Naxi are such gentle people; they are polite and soft spoken, unlike the average aggressive Chinese merchants in Shanghai or Beijing. The shop girl tells Malina that her brother is the artist of these pieces. She points to a young man sitting in a corner of the store who has been quietly working on another piece of art. Malina is delighted and asks whether he would explain the meanings of the carvings to her. Shyly, he introduces himself as Geshu and happily obliges.

Geshu exclaims that Malina must be psychic, that she has picked two interrelated pieces. He first clarifies that his Naxi tribe is from the stars, and that star-people have a special mission on Earth. He proceeds to explain the first carving as two souls who have been separated and who wish to come back together. In the Naxi sacred tradition, the women are always the stronger and the clearer ones with their life missions. They remember their destinies and they are the ones calling their lovers home, with patient determination. That's why the woman's face in the artwork is more prominent at the forefront. However, the men are usually ambiguous and show reluctance to return, because they are ensnared, during their wandering, in the seductive powers of the Moon, which distort their psyche and cloud their minds.

The Naxi legend proclaims, from time immemorial, that the dark forces in the cosmos have been using the Moon, masking its true light in order to control humanity. It is a common perception in the world that the Moon represents divine feminine energy, whereas in truth it vibrates cunning female seduction that tricks the male psyche into its folds. That's why the male face looks sad and trapped. It is up to the divine memory in the woman to remember this alteration of the Moon, to stay un-wavering through the ages, and ultimately bring the man home to his own fullness, thus liberating him and the Moon. It is a story of light over darkness in our beguiling Universe, when love triumphs over manipulation. The Moon yearns for ascension back into its purity as humans long for emancipation from their own bondages.

The second piece of art is the exultant story of *Starseeds* reunited. Through a disciplined cultivation of her sexual kundalini, the woman's crown chakra opens up into a lotus of thousand petals with a divine frequency that transmutes negative vibrations. From the bottomless pool of her tenderness, she beams messages from her eyes into his, which dissolve any foggy memories. His molecules expand as he listens to her with such rapture that a blossoming lotus grows from his ear. They acknowledge their shared essence. Two parts of the whole find their way back to each other and into the stars—uniting with open eyes and hearts in dimensions beyond the finite—thus co-creating their joint lotus, glorious and pure out of murky waters of eons past.

Marveling at the spiritual depth of the young artist Geshu, Malina is immersed in the tales that feel so familiar to her when she hears an exclamation in English behind her: "It's so beautiful! I wish I could understand more of what he said." She whips around and sees an Asian man standing closely behind her, overlooking her shoulders and eying the woodcarvings with admiration. He instinctively backs off a bit and apologizes for crowding her space. She inquires in English, detecting his American accent: "You don't speak Chinese?" He shrugs, looking a bit embarrassed but is relieved that she speaks English: "I'm Chinese, but I was born in America. I can only understand a little. Are you American too?"

She nods and assesses him quickly. He's a handsome man—maybe in his forties or early fifties, with an aura of subdued elegance. He's now intently looking back at her, the mutual magnetism instantaneous. Malina's heart skips a beat; she has never felt immediate recognition of another soul so powerfully before. Everything in her cells screams to her that she *knows* him. She's caught off-guard by feeling drawn to a stranger so suddenly, and she almost blushes. She's confused inside. Geshu is now wrapping her purchases carefully.

The man looks delighted and says: "Oh great, you bought them! Can you explain their meanings to me?" At this time, the artist's sister suggests that the gentleman look at other pieces but he responds innocently: "Your art is beautiful, but I only like these two pieces. Do you have any more of them?" In stilted English, she regretfully says that each sculpture is unique, but her brother can custom-carve for him similar art, if he can wait a week or two. Replying politely that he will think about it, his eyes follow Malina, who is getting ready to leave with her package. "Excuse me for being forward," he says, "May I invite you for a cup of tea? I'd really love to hear the stories of your carvings." He looks anxiously endearing as a little boy. Intuitively sensing that he is harmless, Malina relaxes and smiles at the stranger: "Sure, why not?" She is happy not to have to leave so abruptly after feeling such a familiarity about him.

"My name is Ryan," he stretches out his hand enthusiastically. She holds his warm palm in her fingers: "I'm Malina." After she thanks and praises the artist, they saunter off to a side-street café with lanterns on bamboo poles and outdoor seating, overshadowed by undulating willow trees. Ryan sighs with satisfaction: "I've been here for two weeks now, and I just can't get over the exquisiteness of this town." Malina observes his sensitive use of language. Over fragrant rose-petal tea—a specialty from the high mountains of Yunnan—and some local delicacies, Malina recounts the tales told by Geshu, the artist in the store. Ryan is noticeably moved; Malina detects some almost imperceptible tears in his eyes. She can't help to be amazed that his response to the stories is parallel to her reaction when she first saw the sculptures. She is even more surprised when he indicates innocently that he believes in the star-people, that he has been contemplating the grander scheme of human existence. He himself yearns for true partnership between the sexes in more elevated forms. This sensibility captivates her attention.

Ryan came from a family of high achievers. He is a second generation Chinese-American. Both his parents were highly educated professionals and are now retired. They expected considerable achievements from their children like most Asian parents, but they did not pay much attention to their Chinese lineage. They are thoroughly integrated in the American society, speak very little Chinese and have never encouraged their children to learn the language. Ryan has a brother who's a prominent surgeon in Los Angeles, a sister who's a professor of anthropology in Chicago, and he himself is an entrepreneur in the high-tech trade, working with suppliers in various countries. He now lives in Austin, Texas.

Ryan has realized that he doesn't even know what it's like to be Chinese. His grandparents had migrated to the United States from Yunnan, China a long way back. His parents vaguely remembered they partially have a tribal bloodline coursing through their veins—some ethnic group called Naxi—but they had never taken the time to understand further. That is Ryan's reason for being here, in search of his roots for the first time, through his sister's encouragement. She had done some research for him and Ryan is indeed curious about this ancient indigenous culture.

Ryan feels he cannot be whole without reconciling with some deep aspects of his ancestry. He regrets he has not learned to speak Chinese, and he feels a bit lost not being able to properly communicate with people here, but it doesn't deter him from trying to find echoes of his past. That is why he was so moved when he stumbled into the artisan's shop and saw the star-people's carvings that struck a chord in his heart. Hearing Malina's explanation of the stories has excited him and made him want to know more. He sheepishly asked whether Malina would be his guide to help him deepen his understanding of the cultural nuances. Malina responds positively; she is delighted to have met such a nice companion with whom to share her journey. Malina speaks fluent Chinese. She migrated with her parents and siblings to America from Taiwan when she was a teenager, so her Chinese language foundation was already formed.

Ryan feels at ease with Malina, as though he has known her for a long time. He continues to share his life story. Since his difficult divorce a few years ago, he has been pondering on issues of the human plights and the conflicts of the sexes. He loves and respects women, but he was shocked when his ex-wife, herself highly educated and a software programmer, demanded a huge alimony and displayed behaviors of entitlement when they agreed to terminate their dead-end marriage. Almost all her female friends ganged up against him, as if he had committed a crime, even though the wish to dissolve the marriage was mutual. Ryan has now long recovered from the resentment of the bitter divorce. However, the double standard of privilege espoused by many women who tout woman's liberation astounds him, as he has noticed from his own experience and from those of his male friends. He has since been on a path of self-discovery and soul searching to understand deeper aspects of himself and of the human psyche. He observed how this world is still run by women behind the scenes, manipulating men in myriads of conscious and unconscious ways while disapproving of patriarchy; whereas men blindly congratulate themselves for being in charge, indulging in their unwitting behaviors of domination. Ryan is keenly concerned with examining the subjects of matriarchy and patriarchy without condemnation, but with an interest to discover more balanced ways of existence.

Ryan and Malina are so immersed in swapping life stories that they don't notice time passing. When they lift their heads to look around, the ethereal twilight has enwrapped Lijiang in an otherworldly beauty, with glistening reflections dotting the canals. Eateries and shops are lit up with delicately swaying lanterns—the night scenery of this town has inspired countless poems and literature from travelers around the world. The streets come alive with candlelit restaurants, enhanced with melodies of ancient music played by street musicians sitting by the bridges, and charming coffeehouses boasting fusion cuisine of old and new.

They agree on a simply quaint noodle-house in which to have a bowl of *Crossing The Bridge Rice Noodles* for supper, a delicacy of Yunnan that comes with tiny dishes filled with an assortment of condiments that Ryan loves. He heartily remarks: "I love Chinese food the best, there are so many varieties!"

After dinner, they stroll down meandering bridges and linger to watch a group of Naxi men and women dancing in a circle, a ritual dance around a roaring fire to praise nature that they regularly gather to do, for one spiritual celebration or another. The performers are mainly older people in the inner ring, with youngsters on the outer ring, while elderly male musicians play with uniquely carved ancient instruments. Their joyous ambiance must have stimulated Ryan, for he spontaneously jumps in, motioning for Malina to join him. She chooses to remain with the observing crowd and just watches his jubilation. He is transported to another time—he dances uninhibitedly as though he has always danced with these tribal rhythms. Malina's heart melts; even this sweet feeling seems familiar to her. When Ryan returns to her side, he is sweaty and excited: "My god, I've never danced like this before! I feel so at home with these people!"

Their melding together is as natural as a gentle breeze hugging their hearts. Ryan and Malina spend the subsequent weeks together without any pretense or excuses, exploring and discovering the magic of the Naxi people, and each other. Ryan has rented a charming little villa, decorated with Naxi antiquities, on the outskirts of town. Instead of her room in the heart of the old town square, they prefer to luxuriate for hours in the serene quietude of his place to nurture their newfound love. While snuggled in his embrace, Malina is carried back to ancient times, her heart opening to glimpses of remembrance of a far-away land.

She feels immeasurable delight of being beautiful for him, and for herself. She welcomes his erotic expressions that are reflections of her own. The fluidity of their mutual arousal echoes lifetimes of reciprocated recognition. They delve into secret nooks of pleasure of each other's bodies without tentative probing or hesitation. They conjoin as clouds and rain, caressing each other as soft wind does the land.

When she holds his throbbing wand in her hands, savoring his delectable scent, rubbing it against her nose, her cheeks, and brushing it against her nipples, she has the gratifying sensation of having played with this sacred flute for eons. This act of love always provokes an electrifying response from Ryan, who in turn indulges Malina endlessly by worshipping her lush garden in a hundred ways that spark spine-tingling shivers in her. Ryan enfolds her with so much adoring love that her valley of Eden keeps beckoning for more, opening both of them up in heart and body that burst through gates of paradise.

These pulsating moments of bliss only ignite in them further feelings of a devoted love through time immemorial. They together are a living, breathing manifestation of a mystical past. Their resonant vibration dissolves the veils of separation, melts the sorrows of longing that their hearts have carried for years. It is a synergy of pure essence that each drinks from the other's well. Nothing is in the way of the sacred expressions they offer to each other. Malina told Ryan the auspicious premonition of the elderly woman on the plane.

They feel anchored in each other; their hearts merge in a unified field of wedded memories. Their coming together is as unerring as the renewing springtime. The blossoming petals of the lotus unfold between them. Their grateful hearts know that the Naxi sculpture of the *Starseeds reunited* was a coded portal to bring them back together. They now have coalesced back into oneness, they are home at last.

Ryan continues to share more of his inner self. He confides to Malina that he has been patiently waiting for his mirror to appear. He knows that he has first to become whole in himself—living the fullness of masculine and feminine within— before his equal would emerge. He no longer wants to be shackled by resentment or fear of living an unheralded humdrum life; he is ready to take on the world with love and compassion. He doesn't want to make excuses to shun life anymore because of its despairs and corruptions. He currently places much more commitment to his spiritual path than building his financial portfolio. The amassing of wealth and success no longer excites him. He has been more focused on his inner life these last few years.

He studied intensely with a Lama from Tibet; he joined men's groups and vision quests. He experimented for a long period with ayahuasca—the sacred medicine from the Amazons used by shamans for revelations of the mysteries of the Universe—which has thoroughly changed his life. He is a richer man internally because of the depth and breadth—the light and deep-seated shadows of himself that were exposed to him—that he confronted with his naked soul and humility. It has been challenging and hard work, at times even agonizing, to face himself in all aspects of his own convolution. Once he stepped on the path of truth seeking, there was no way of return. He is becoming a better human being for himself.

Malina is enthralled with his ease and directness. He is clearly a man comfortable in his own skin. He displays neither affectations nor grandiosity in sharing of his spiritual growth and discoveries. He believes in it without making apologies. It was through the visions of ayahuasca that Ryan realized he and many others were star-people who had come to Earth from other planets and star systems. They have been here for epochs in search of truth, and to merge the worlds. Though many remain stuck in tormenting conflicts or in self-glorifying acts of darkness, there are also many like him who continue to burst through the cloaks of materialism that have hypnotically numbed down the human spirit for ages.

Ryan saw and experienced moments of eternal bliss that emanated from within and he was euphorically yearning for more during those cosmic journeys. He feels intensely in the core of his cellular memories that he is here in this lifetime to be a change agent—a warrior of peace—and not of battle. He perseveres in challenging every aspect of himself to become the will and courage to let go of stereotypical masculine persona and roles of outdated collective values. Yet he feels dejected at times at not knowing how to help change the collective, stuck in its self-inflicted quagmires. The American economy is in shambles, the world becomes more chaotic with fears for survival looming larger than ever. What can he do to make a difference?

Ryan has decided to change one person at a time, beginning with himself. He knows it is not enough to realize who he is underneath his personality; it is what he does with it in life that defines his spiritual maturity. He recognizes that darkness cannot rule when the radiant light is burning within every human being. The key is to unlock the jail door to self-imprisonment— the cell of self-tortured smallness. Ryan believes in the hundredth-monkey effect. He feels that humanity is poised to come together to usher in the age of Oneness. He has patiently encouraged his male friends, whoever are willing to listen, to join in a self-committed pathwork, no matter what spiritual roads they take.

Malina loves listening to him. There is an impeccable virtue, a fiery glow in his being when his penetrating eyes flash with strength, vitality and humor. She relaxes into an infinite gratitude that the greater forces have united them back into one heart, at the eleventh hour of the ending of *logical time* of the linear mind, as prophesied by the Mayan Calendar. She knows they are poised on the threshold of a more fluid inter-dimensional time and space of original creativity through equal partnership, of Unity Consciousness that will flourish for millennia to come. They are propelled by a new forcefield of synchronic timing to align their common purpose in life, naturally moving into a synergized intention to serve the greater whole. It is *Divine Will* that they are destined to be rainbows bridging East and West, to help bring the beauty of equilibrium into all fields of inner evolution. *Balance* is the fundamental wisdom of their Chinese lineage, and it flows naturally through their way of being. Malina feels an infinite gratitude for this innate compatibility between them.

Ryan and Malina continue to unearth with keen interest the mysteries of the Naxi culture together. With her translation of the language and her pointing out to him the deeper perspectives of their various cultural encounters, Ryan gains profound insights into his own being. He realizes that he is the embodiment of East and West, regardless of the language barrier, which now merges in harmony within him. He feels more complete than ever before.

They travel to the Luoshui village around Lugu lake where the Mosuo tribal community still maintains its prehistoric matrilineal structure and the ancient "walk-in" marital ritual. The lock in Ryan's heart—whatever cellular memory of antipathy toward matriarchy or lopsided female power—is liberated. They listen with delight as an elderly shaman sings to them, in the ancient DongBa language, the wisdom of this culture that ebbs and flows with nature. As the shaman invites them to his niece's family to share a simple meal of spicy fish, wild mushroom, taro and rice cakes in vinegar, the timeless ambience of the harmonious household touches a deep chord in both their hearts. They watch as Naxi women nearby peacefully tend to their livestock, and young men in amiable collaboration carve birds into wooden windows of a humble dwelling. It moves them deeply to feel into the hearts of these people who intermingle in peace with the land, living out their implicit treaty with nature.

Malina silently hands a card to Ryan, which she prepared the day before they arrived in Luoshui. He takes his time to appreciate the hand-made paper with the pictorial DongBa scriptures on the front side—he is so proud to have learned of the written sophistication of his heritage. It was the Naxi people, thousands of years ago, who had first invented acid-free paper, using natural fibers from plants. His ancestors believe that everything in nature has a soul; even paper is slowly cooked and stirred into being with love. Ryan opens the card and tears fill his eyes as he reads T. S. Eliot's poem in Malina's handwriting. The words so poignantly describe his sentiment of the moment, which he knows is hers also, as he gazes into the quiet wisdom reflected in Malina's eyes:

> We shall not cease from exploration
> And the end of all our exploring
> Will be to arrive where we started
> And know the place for the first time.

Love of a Pharaoh

In pure hearted loving, the DNA triangulation is awakened
—an alchemy that unlocks cosmic memories.

Love of a Pharaoh

IT WAS Sara's second day in Cairo and she was enchanted by her experiences thus far. For years she had felt a deep connection to Egypt, though she had not delved into any profound soul inquiries as to why. She finally joined a group of some thirty spiritual seekers from different countries, led by an author named Alena, who had written books on transcendent consciousness and who seemed to know a lot about the mystical intrigues of this country.

The group was treated to a lavish Egyptian feast on the first welcome-and-get-acquainted evening, then a day tour of the city, and a shopping frenzy at the bazaars. Sara was fascinated by the cacophony of jostling merchants, the arrays of galabiyas and kaftans, the multi-colored shisha glass pipes, the countless fake antiques, and the glittering variety of silver jewelry. She noticed the soothing drone of chanting from the nearby mosque, which was quite a contrast to the feverish clatters of the bazaar. Egyptian men aggressively approached tourist-women with marriage proposals and seductive compliments, while hustling them in the same breath to buy trinkets. As Sara meandered about, local men appraised her and commented that she looked like an Egyptian princess. She got more marriage proposals in two days than in her entire adult life! Thank goodness she felt safe with the group while zigzagging through the dazzling alleys overflowing with Egyptian cotton wear, souvenirs and unending knick-knacks.

Sara was a Eurasian with deep-set brown eyes, from which green-gold flecks effervesced, especially when she smiled, but she never thought she looked Mediterranean. Maybe it was because of her almost black hair and her rather olive skin that some locals mistook her for being an Egyptian.

This evening, Alena took the group to a light show in a famous temple but Sara opted to spend a meditative evening in her room, hoping for an early night's sleep, since they were going to meet at six o'clock the next morning for a visit to the Great Pyramid. Alena specifically planned this event to take place on the very day of the Spring Equinox, on March twenty-first. Sara was excited about this auspicious date; she had longed to experience this great monument first-hand after reading so much about its grandeur and mysteries through the years. She drifted into sleep very quickly. It was one of those groggy, jet-lagged slumbers that tumbled her through surreal, yet lucid visions.

A Pharaoh came to her. He was bare-chested, devoid of any pompous headdress or jewelry. He was simply wrapped in a white kilt with a gold sash, and sporting a pair of unadorned gold sandals. The aura of light and splendor that emanated from his deep dark eyes and his angular face was unmistakably regal. He was handsome in a strange way, with prominent cheekbones on a long thin face and sensuous thick lips. He had an unusually tall and taut body, with a bit of a protruding belly—quite an odd combination. Sara somehow knew that he was a descendant of the Sun God, Horus.

In the dream, she was not the Sara of this lifetime. Instead she was a lovely young maiden, not a queen or even a consort of the King's harem. She was chosen by the high priests to be devoted to a single task: to be made love to by the Pharaoh for a sublime mission, which presumably would affect the distant future of humankind. Her rendezvous with the Pharaoh regularly happened in a ritual room with only one bed, decorated with finely carved urns and sacred amulets, and dimly lit by a few oil lamps. The room was always prepared with reverence by the temple priests, who dowsed it with heavenly scented oils combined with a single piece of frankincense smoldering in a gold incense burner. As a ceremonial prelude, she was bathed in a sacred pool by female attendants incanting celestial chants of love. Then they oiled her with a secret blend of aromas that she revered, which put her in a trance-like state. She was dressed simply in a translucent white flowing long skirt, cinched with a belt glimmering with small crystals. There were no adornments in her lustrous black hair. She was also bare-chested, ornamented with only a beaded necklace that dropped between her breasts, and culminated in a large, dark blue labradorite crystal pendant. It was iridescent with a rainbow of brilliant hues, and was used for the invocation of Earth magic and divination. She waited in silent purity.

The Pharaoh came to her and greeted her with joyous respect; he did not require her to prostrate to him. She was his sacred equal in their task of divine union. After they sipped a libation that was carefully prepared by the priests who then quietly exited, he tenderly kissed the delicate features of her face and slowly coiled his tongue in each of her ears, arousing her.

He then sensually fondled her body, cupping her voluptuous breasts with both of his hands worshipfully. He gently suckled each of her juicy nipples, exciting her.

He slowly ran his tongue round and round her smooth skin above her navel, which ignited unbearable desire in her. The Pharaoh leisurely moved downward and found her bud of flesh in erection and he kissed it while slowly licking the clear liquid that moistened her jewel. He tended to the most sensitive part and stimulated it until it swelled out and became inflamed. His fingers ran along the rosy folds of her lotus, ruffled her lustrous dark triangle, tickled the sensitive flesh of her inner thighs, and then his hands pushed her legs further apart. Briskly he turned her over with a powerful grip on her supple waist, brought her buttocks tight against his tautly erect phallus, and unfastened her long skirt.

The Pharaoh proceeded to sensually caress her delicate and graceful back with his long fingers. He passionately thrust himself inside of her from behind, his movements made easy by the flow of her moistness, pulsating and expanding with such potent vigor that it sent intoxicating sparks throughout her body. He stirred back and forth with long and penetrating strokes. He felt mighty as a slithering herculean serpent inside of her, at the same time he massaged her breasts so erotically that it prompted more nectar to drip down her thighs. She moaned with rapture and they climaxed together in one powerful explosion!

As his throbbing subsided inside of her, the Pharaoh held her in a tender embrace, and whispered in her ears: "When a man loves a woman with a purity of heart and with an abandon of bodily release, he stimulates a DNA triangulation in her energetic field, transducing the double helix with a third strand. This strand is of an etheric nature, transmitting and receiving cosmic information on the blueprint of the human genetic origin. This triangulation catalyzes the harmonic frequencies of the universe and calibrates the cellular waters of her body. These waters are the divine conductor of all cosmic knowing within." Trance-like, he infused her with knowledge, as he did every time after their lovemaking.

The Pharaoh told her that someday in the future, it would be her sacred duty to impart this wisdom to humanity. "The human body itself has a complete trinity circuitry, represented by the grid of the two nipples to the genitalia. By animating these sacred areas with conscious loving, a man brings a woman into an orgasmic liberation of her life force. This in turn feeds him with an injection of vitality, which then induces his ejaculation that explodes into energetic light codes up her spine, thus completing a magical ring. The DNA triangulation results in the alchemy of a divine nectar which unlocks both of their cosmic memories."

While running his hand along her curvy hips, the Pharaoh reflected with melancholy, "Through the ages, priests and kings alike would try in vain to obtain this essence from women whom they thought have stolen it from their life force. Therefore they would validate sacrificing virgins and amass harems in order to find this elusive fluid. Earthly religions would elucidate this quest as the Holy Grail, a myth for which they would search and kill in futility. Emperors, philosophers, and conquistadors, on the other hand, would claim to have visions of an eternal fountain of youth that would lead to justification of utter violence toward one another. They would conquer lands and massacre indigenous people the world over in an attempt to find this mysterious well for their longevity. What they would not know is that this elixir can only be preciously co-created by the sacred love between a man and a woman, leading to life eternal. Only in union through pure love can this nectar be alchemized." The Pharaoh looked deep into her eyes and spoke, "Love is not a mere feeling. Love is the *Breath of Oneness*. It is the all-emanating energy that shines from the core of creation itself." Oh, how she adored the wisdom and the tenderhearted love of her Pharaoh.

He stroked her back affectionately and continued: "Our union encodes this knowledge in your spine. It serves as a holographic patterning that sends light pulses to preset your inner circuitry, which reside in your cellular memories from lifetime to lifetime. The human spine is the cosmic ladder connecting Heaven and Earth; it is the divine vessel of the ultimate serpent power. It contains all the wisdom of the DNA's interstellar codes. Humans never need to search outside of themselves. It is simply through *Oneness in Love* that they will recall themselves as light particles, divided into male and female forms to experience the binary, then by choice to remember themselves back into the light. Until the understanding of this divine coding is thoroughly integrated and manifested through human love, there will always be war and strife amongst men and women, countries, and cultures."

Sara woke up suddenly in a daze, shaken-up, and her body still tingling sexually by the Pharaoh's astral visitation. She felt overwhelmed by the concise communication in her dream state. She seemed to intuitively comprehend the transmission well just a moment ago, yet it was too complex for her to fully grasp it now that she was awake, especially the part about DNA triangulation and the concept of light codes. She thought science discovered DNA in the 1900s; how did the Pharaoh know about it in his time? Then she realized that the mysteries of humanity had long been understood by ancient wisdom and that his delivery to her must have purposely been conveyed in the language and words that she could understand. Sara quickly grabbed her diary on the nightstand and wrote down as much as she remembered. However, what was she supposed to do with this information?

The next morning her group was shuttled to the Giza Plateau and was swiftly ushered inside the Great Pyramid as part of a private excursion due to Alena's special connection to some local authority, without having to be herded along with flocks of tourists. It was an awesome feeling for Sara to go down into the eerie subterranean level with only rickety planks as stairways, and then slowly up to the famous King's Chamber, where no king had ever actually resided. It was purported to be the room for cosmic initiation for the likes of Jesus Christ and Napoleon Bonaparte. Alena allotted each person two to three minutes to lie down inside the dark red sarcophagus, while she intoned an invocation to support any intention-making meditation.

When it was Sara's turn, she was almost reluctant to get in the gigantic granite tub. Her sensitive nose picked up pungent foul odors—the legacy of hundreds of years of looting and desecration in this sacred room. She lay down uneasily and her mind went blank. She wasn't prepared with any purpose. As she closed her eyes, a voice suddenly came over her: "You have promised for eons to write about ending the division of the sexes. This is the time. Will you make your pledge now?" She was stunned by this declaration that came out of nowhere; she felt disoriented and nodded a timid yes, got up, and was helped out of the tub by Alena. She joined the group in chanting and holding space for the rest of the people going into the sarcophagus one by one, while she was overcome with emotions. Tears streamed down Sara's face; she was on the edge of remembering that long-ago promise, pouring forth from the recesses of her memories.

The rest of the day flew by like a dream. Though Sara enjoyed touring the Sphinx and meditating at the base of its awe-inspiring paws, her mind was transfixed by the command inside the Pyramid, which linked synchronistically to her vision of the night before. But who was she to write on such a lofty subject? She was still a single woman who has had disappointing and heart-wrenching relationships through the years. What did she have to say that could be enlightening after thousands of published treatises and theories had expounded on the battles of the sexes? Nonetheless, she also knew humanity today was still pathetically clueless on this elusive and unsolved challenge. But how was she going to convince anybody that a love nectar could solve the warring problems of the world?!

The next day, her group was shuttled to Edfu, the temple of Horus. Sara was looking forward to visiting inside the temple, hoping to find a trace of her Pharaoh on one of the bas-reliefs. As she passed by two gigantic columns outside the temple, she was mesmerized by the Sun's radiance. She felt as though some force field was rendering her immobile. Sara vaguely remembered Alena saying that they would have thirty minutes inside the temple and would need to reconvene outside at the main entrance afterward. Sara knew that she could rejoin her group later, so she relaxed and surrendered into this strange phenomenon. Though swarms of tourists strode in and out of her path and her peripheral vision, Sara wasn't self-conscious.

In an entranced pose, she outstretched her arms toward the Sun, eyes wide open, hypnotized by its beckoning. She was instantly infused with a huge column of liquid crystals in diamond brilliance, beaming directly into her whole body from the center of the Sun, penetrating every fiber of her being, as though re-configuring her DNA structure. She knew in that moment that she was being initiated in some mystical way by the Sun. Two gargantuan golden ET faces split off from the Sun, with enormous eyes and pointy chins, bestowing benevolence and joyfulness upon her. Sara then saw a perfectly iridescent rainbow encircling the rim of the Sun. The splendor of this sight took her breath away. More ETs were gamboling and leaping about, diverging in all directions to becoming human souls. They all looked like the Egyptian Ankhs; then they became human-like stick figures, scattered across the sky. 'Maybe that was how Egyptians surmised the Ankh to be the symbol of eternal life?' Sara wondered. A multitude of circles and geometric patterns shot out from the blinding shards of the Sun; perhaps this was the original inspiration for the myriad shapes of intricate architecture throughout ancient cultures. Kaleidoscopic forms, contours, tablets, and hieroglyphic codes sprang all at once from the rays. There were serpent-like shapes writhing down; Sara felt she was given a revelation of the primordial formation of humanity on planet Earth.

Sara continued to stare into the Sun, eyes wide open, for a seemingly endless time, letting it charge and infuse her with light, though not comprehending how that could be possible in the high Sun of egyptian heat. Normally she wouldn't be able to look into the Sun for more than a couple of seconds without being blinded by its brilliance. She felt an orgasmic euphoria of light exploding throughout her body from the liquid sunshine, while golden poles and liquescent crystals showered upon her. It dawned on Sara that the colossal architectural columns around the world must have been inspired by the Sun's pillars of light, no matter the civilizations. People of the old cultures must have tuned into similar cosmic visions.

The Sun's majestic voice suddenly resounded in her head: "The power of the male organ is a microcosm of me. The phallus is an encoded shaft of light. When a man enters a woman's sacredness, he is my essence penetrating the crystalline womb of Earth. Earth is my beloved; we have agreed to a cosmic destiny of union to co-create life in the 3-dimensional. She stores my light with ecstasy, generates and propagates life through time immemorial for all living forms." The Sun then revealed to Sara that ultimately, the evolution of human consciousness would depend on the appreciation of the *Great Love* between him and the Earth, his everlasting fertilization of her mysterious and receptive layers. Humanity's willingness to embrace this practice of consecrated alchemy in their lives would transform the meaning of their sexual union to a higher evolution of being. Needless to say, this assertion astounded Sara and yet it felt natural to her.

Sara felt reborn into the knowing and she was elated. She reveled in allowing the liquid gold inside of her to reconstruct her very being, surrendering to the magic she was experiencing. Then she was totally wiped out for the rest of the day, she went in and out of a trance state. She was a bit concerned about her foolishness in staring at the Sun for so long, and wondered if her eyes were somehow permanently damaged. She was also troubled that she kept having sexual visions and messages, first from the Pharaoh and now from the Sun. Had she been so lonely without a lover for so long that her subconscious consoled her with these fantasies?

Sara was overwhelmed by the profound communications she received, one day after another, and couldn't integrate it all. She generally remained silent or quietly smiling during the group social functions in order to mask her internal turbulence. Though her fellow travelers were no spiritual newcomers, she felt too vulnerable and didn't know anyone well enough to share the uncanny events she had experienced. The next few days flew by like a whirlwind. Though she delighted in visiting the impressive Karnak, Isis, Hathor and Hatshepsut temples, and learning about each of their unique legends and history, many of the explanations given by the Egyptologist hired by Alena did not ring true to her. All the devouring gods, jealous goddesses, conflicts and intrigues, wars and captures recorded for millennia, were boring regurgitations of superstitions and of the conquerors' tales that did not touch her heart. As her group cruised down the Nile— the archetypal spine of this fascinating land of wisdom, Sara mused on a different kind of knowing that was innately familiar to her—the kind imparted to her by the Pharaoh and the Sun.

As she wandered through the endless parade of

sculpted murals in the Valley of the Kings, she longed to find a visual resemblance of the Pharaoh who visited her in her dreams, but many of the kings' faces were either damaged or mutilated. The ancient Egyptian culture had a wicked habit of chiseling off the features of nobles when they fell out of political favor. Besides, the effigies were blemished from time and erosion. She went to the Cairo museum to peruse through historical books, looking for her Pharaoh. The one who resembled him from her veiled memory was none other than Akhenaten, the heretic king who had overturned all the old religions to worship the single Sun deity Aten, and declared himself *Son of the Sun*. He had only a short reign of seventeen years during the 18th dynasty, before his mysterious death. 'That would make sense,' mused Sara, since the Sun's revelations to her at Edfu were connected to the Pharaoh's teachings. Sara was intimidated though to think that one of her previous lives could be related to Akhenaten. After all, this great Pharaoh's famous queen was the magnificent Nefertiti!

She went to bed every night asking the Pharaoh to come to her in visions again; she was burning with so many questions. He finally appeared toward the end of her trip, clad in the familiar simple garb, and with so much tender love on his face. Sara in the dreams asked him urgently whether he was Akhenaten and he only gently smiled at her saying, "My love, it doesn't matter who I am in a man's body, I am the cosmic light of creation." Bathed in such radiance and clarity, she felt puerile to even be curious about any earthly attachments she might condone in her fantasy. She was once again transformed into that young beauty, anticipating and surrendering to her sacred task.

Her Pharaoh lay on the bed, relaxed and amorous. He lovingly took her hand to arouse his nipples, while he was teasing hers. He slowly helped her to grasp his aroused member and guided her movements. He telepathically exhorted her to fully concentrate on the enjoyment of the exquisite sensations he was feeling, transmitting to her the tempo and cadence of his erection, speeding up or slowing down, following the building up of his excitement until she took charge of synchronizing their pleasures. It was a strangely new awareness, but she went along as a dutiful apprentice, and let the vibrations emanate. In the throes of a highly orgasmic state, she erupted into climax, feeling intense waves of pleasure in her nipples and genitals, but she was experiencing these pulsations as if she were the

Pharaoh, enjoying his body being stimulated. Amazed by this phenomenon, she thoroughly felt his pleasure spreading throughout her body, while he seemed to be responding with her expressions and feelings of ecstasy. They both fell into a tsunami of unstoppable delight, becoming one.

As the Pharaoh massaged her indulgently, he resumed his teaching: "Each of us is complete with a trinity in our own body, but when the energies are merged and exchanged—like what we just experienced earlier—the union is sublime, and it will lead to layers of healing between men and women. Men need to feel safe enough to relax into receiving physical and emotional pleasures without always being the instigating forces. It is essential for women to bestow sexual love wholeheartedly without manipulating men for their own conditional purposes, no matter how innocent their motivations might seem."

"However" exclaimed the Pharaoh, "most of humankind is not conscious of the sacred body triangulation, especially men. Many are unaware of the sensitivity in their nipples. The sensations in them are underdeveloped and have mostly gone dormant without loving stimulations. Deprived of the full awareness on how they can feel the divine pleasure within themselves, men are numbed down and resort to aggressive behaviors towards one another. They subjugate women because they unconsciously remember the heavenly richness of ecstasy, which they can never get enough of from women. The missing link is from within; yet they get frustrated in not being able to gracefully access the divine state. Men keep hungering after women and yet are terrified of the female power that seems to govern their emotions. So their self-defense turns into controlling or abusive conducts. The denseness of patriarchal bearings will rule for some thousand years, unfortunately."

He looked pensive and continued, "One day, in another life when the right timing comes due, you will meet a lover who resonates in body, mind and spirit with you. He is your mirror. When your physical triangulations are interlocked during love's pleasures, you activate together the complete circuitry of the *Six Pointed Star*—the cosmic creation code of spirit grounded in matter. The paradise of harmonious embrace through divine union is the infinite state of *love* transduced by *light*. Humans are the embodiments of the intersected Sun and Earth—the upright male pyramid and its inverted female counterpart joining each other to form the sacred geometry of union, transmuting duality into an ascended state of celestial consciousness."

The young maiden asked softly, "Will my lover be an incarnation of you, my king?" The Pharaoh smiled with wisdom and infinite patience as he kissed her lips. "He will be a fractal aspect of my emanation. He is my essence, as I am an essence of the Sun. He will have an undeniable presence, forever fearless in his questing, with an indomitable spirit in pursuing the truth of his destiny, even when he seems to resist it and stumble now and again." The Pharaoh became excited again and he pushed his hard shaft up against her. He continued, "Your lover will epitomize the reason why men love through physical penetration—because all men carry the matrix of the Sun, which is the ultimate architect in this galaxy, who delights in creating forms by penetrating the depths of Earth from which life springs forth. As for you, my love, you represent the quintessence of Earth, and will inspire women back into the remembrance of weaving emotional oneness with her. You will embody the regenerative power of life itself, through manifesting agelessness with your beloved." The Pharaoh then sensuously entered her and loved her with an unbridled primal passion, that of divine consciousness itself. Sara, as the maiden in the dream, felt the jubilant merging of Heaven and Earth flowing through them. They became complete in each other.

"Many divinely intended couples such as the two of you would be called upon to rejoin together—after many lifetimes of separation—in order to deliver celestial expressions through sacred union. Each couple has pledged to fulfill a specific cosmic task. Your work with your beloved will be to stir humanity to remember how to re-awaken their physical and energetic DNA triangulations and how to live the true meaning of the *Six Pointed Star* with reverence. Sacred love happens when two human beings are whole and complete within themselves. When true love triumphs beyond bondage and beyond limited concepts of romantic love, Unity Consciousness naturally flourishes. Love is not complete without honoring sexuality in its sanctified state of exultation. This conscious coupling becomes an all-encompassing love that brings about the foundation of a *Greater Reality*."

The Pharaoh gently caressed her body, "When you

and your lover unite as a couple, you will instantly recognize each other through your first sexual encounter, for you will have been together in many lifetimes. You will ignite in each other a knowingness of this memory. His love will touch you to the very core of your being and re-kindle your spinal wisdom. Your love will re-awaken in him his sacred destiny. When that time comes, it will not be a smooth and easy road. There will be many tests of separation and heart-breaking trials of faltering love with others, conditioned by the binary human plight. But through perseverance and trust in your soul love, you will eventually reunite to manifest your holy mission, bringing sacred sexuality to the forefront, and helping to end the disunion between the sexes. Men are to live as emanations of the Sun's radiance; women are to manifest the living ambrosia of Earth, melding all opposites into *Oneness*."

The Pharaoh then sympathetically and solemnly held her face, "Only then will the abuses of this planet cease and humanity rise to a new conscious equilibrium. Earth will be healed and fully awakened to her ascension dance with the Sun, leading humanity out of its self-inflicted quagmires and conflicts." He longingly kissed her goodbye with tender love and kindness before he faded away.

Sara woke up sobbing with emotions, her tears soaking the pillows. She instinctively knew who the Pharaoh was referring to—Jeremy, the love of her life, with whom she had experienced this exquisitely divine love. The way they adored each other sexually and emotionally, with a soul affinity that transcended this realm of existence, was a once in a lifetime occurrence for her. But challenges in life had separated them for more than fifteen years now. When they were in their younger years with rather fragile psyches, Jeremy and Sara were overwhelmed by life's trials and tribulations that seemed contradictory to their passionate cauldron of love. They did not have the maturity they needed to behold and navigate the fires of the path of spirit. Though no other men in her life had been able to replace Jeremy in her heart, Sara had no idea how to even locate him now. But for the first time since their parting, she had hope in the miracle of destiny.

On the last day of their journey, Alena surprised the group by inviting Hammu, one of the last descendants of the Pharaohs, to talk to them about his perspective on the mysterious grandeur of his lineage. He enigmatically chose to speak about the meanings of the words *Sa* and *Ra* that were of significance to his culture. *Sa*—the God particle that the ancient Egyptians called the 'Sa of life'—was the quintessential elixir that flowed through god-like beings and emanated eternal life through them. *Ra*, of course, was the all-glorious Sun God, who incarnated in various disguises throughout eternity to remind humanity of his inherent fusion with the love energy of Earth. When Sara realized that her own name carried the insignia of these two words, she was dumbfounded. There were so many layers and interwoven revelations on this journey. The synchronicity of events during this pilgrimage was overwhelming to her. This ancient land to which she innately felt such a deep connection, had now perhaps revealed unexpected secrets of a distant past.

When she returned to Seattle, her dear friend Anitah was at the airport to pick her up. She exitedly handed a surprise present to Sara. Anitah was a uniquely gifted *Soul Reader* poet; she had the propensity of tuning into people's souls in her dream state. She woke up one morning and vividly remembered a dream about the reason why Sara went to Egypt. Anitah said she jumped out of bed and wrote down in one breath this poem, which she had just given Sara:

RENDEZVOUS

The spirit of her guardian spirit
Walks darkly in night's silent deep
Resolutely laden with earth-raising destiny.

She ceaselessly holds the millennial secrets
Until the one-she-is-now can claim the mystery
From the one-she-used-to-be.

Standing strong in steeled integrity
The spirit of her steadfast spirit
Fearlessly scans the vast unknown
This watcher of the eras
This holder of the hope.

When she returns to dream-dipped kingdoms
To the courtyards of forgotten gods
The spirit of her knowing spirit
Faithful in service, ripe with time
Surrenders to this awaited one
She who is encoded with command.

And the spirit of her unbound spirit
Fades with the uniting dawn
Finally to rest in triumphant honor
With the one who kept her word.

Sara was beyond stunned holding the poem in her hand as she dissolved in tears of gratitude toward her friend who had, without a clue of the events of the last two weeks in Egypt, independently confirmed the mystery of a past that was submerged in the recesses of Sara's cellular memory. Her heart was in prostration to the Magic of the Divine. She had undeniably journeyed back in time to retrieve a piece of her long-forgotten self. What would happen in the future was up to destiny's hand leading the way.

The Shaman's Ecstasy

As entwined tresses in a euphoric kundalini dance,
the Earth-Queen guides him to weave the straws
in impeccable braided cables.

The Shaman's Ecstasy

DAMIAN was huddled over a prototype, trying to focus on solving the problem at hand. His chief engineer Richard and two technicians stood by him, scratching their heads about the mechanical impasse they had come to. It was a beautiful Sunday afternoon; each one of them would rather have been somewhere else than sweating in the machine shop in which they test-ran Damian's inventions. His latest was the development of a breathable and versatile green building material using residual agricultural wastes such as hemp, rice and wheat straws. This product would be easier to maneuver and of a much smaller size than straw bales, with superior insulation and more seismic strength than the conventional building materials. It had taken him over two years of endless hours and dedication to get to this point, and now he was stumped.

Damian was passionate about preserving the natural world. He was a technology inventor, and he had been having moderate success over the years, creating practical commodities that were eco-friendly. He owned a small R&D company that relied on funding from various grants or from the occasional business people who cared enough about the environment and who wanted to do something good for it. Damian felt uninspired at the moment. His mind was distracted. An inner voice kept nudging him to get out of the shop and commune with nature instead of forcing himself to come up with solutions he has yet to find. Abruptly he told the guys he had to leave. Everyone was used to his quirky moods; and, anyway, they were happy to be dismissed to enjoy whatever was left of Sunday.

Damian drove to nearby woods and stepped out eagerly. He breathed in the pristine air with a sigh of contentment. His spirit was immediately lifted. Nothing was more invigorating to him than being enwrapped in the bosom of the wild. He loved loosing himself for hours just listening to the secret languages of the wind. That was how he always revitalized himself from the pressure of work. As he crunched through the fallen branches and meandered along a bubbling stream, he caught sight of a fairy-like presence whizzing by, skipping furtively through the trees. He quickened his steps to follow it, but it disappeared. Yet he sensed eyes watching him, as though taunting his heightened curiosity. He intensified his search. Then he saw her— an ethereal apparition in evanescent green flowing veils, shrouded by the bushes near the big oaks, but then she vanished as quickly as she appeared. Damian's heart was pounding hard; he wanted desperately to catch another glimpse of her. He thought excitedly: 'I knew it! I knew she would come again!'

When he had been a boy of six or seven, a beautiful woman in shimmering green visited him frequently in his dreams. He always felt safe and reassured by her smile that rippled oceans of love. He somehow knew she was the Queen of the Land and that she presided over all of nature. That sense of wonder and connectedness with the natural world remained with him throughout his adult life. Damian felt lucky that he grew up near open land and lush forests where his parents chose to make their home. During his teenage years, he often felt the Nature Queen whisper to him through the running brooks; enchant him with changing colors on the leaves when summer turned to fall; woo him to doze off in breezy afternoons when he was safely ensconced between her voluptuous round boulders; and delight him with the magic of fireflies in the vastness of the night. He dreamed of stars and exalted lovers.

However, Damian had not seen the Earth Queen in physical form since his younger years when he became fascinated with gadgets and distracted by girls. Then adulthood set in. His pre-occupations with making a living and yielding to the mundane took over, however reluctantly he acquiesced to it. Yet she had always remained close to his heart. Over the years, the Nature Queen whispered to him in soundless wisdom during his many nights of solitude by the campfire, silently guiding and grooming him to listen to the calls of the wild. Being so attuned to nature, Damian was inevitably disgusted by the insatiable greed of business behaviors of mass consciousness.

He chose not to participate in the pursuit of material follies. Instead he had effortlessly honed into some psychic abilities that had helped resolve many perplexing or unpleasant situations in people's lives. Damian was dubbed a *nature mystic,* who assisted people in healing their physiological or psychological ills by tapping into various species in nature as aids or tuning forks. After these healings, Damian needed open space and a lot of alone time to shake off any accumulated negative vibrations that might have clung onto him.

His life unsurprisingly became that of a loner. He made attempts at relationships, but few women understood his yearnings or could fill his heart. He even got married once for a few years trying to normalize his life, but to no avail. Somehow love in the man-made reality was always too confining, too selfish for him. No women could love him as the Earth Queen did, whose tender wisdom and acceptance of who he was extended into boundless wonders of feelings and allowed limitless inner discoveries. He did feel lonely for a woman's touch at times, but, to nourish his soul, he took solace in tinkering with his inventions and trekking unendingly through wilderness.

Imagine Damian's thrill when he came upon a forest sprite so unexpectedly that day. The wind had picked up, but he kept wandering deeper into the dense foliage in pursuit of the alluring phantom. Without warning, a high wind swooshed him into a whirling funnel of churning leaves, and he fell miles and miles in rotating motions into a vortex of a formidable cyclone. He heard a loud thump, and Damian found himself in a place so phantasmagoric that he thought he was in some enchanted dreamland.

Massive and jagged crystals in outrageous formations and colors protruded out from every corner. He reverently fell to his knees with gaping mouth in front of such grandeur. The air felt cool and exhilarating, vibrating an otherworldly frequency that penetrated him like waves of soothing balm. Damian suddenly felt an electrifying presence surrounding him and when he looked up, a goddess-like lady cloaked in iridescent green-gold chiffons had materialized out of nowhere, yet she possessed that same elf-like quality in her eyes that he had spotted through the woods earlier. A sense of awe overtook him in the presence of such regal yet primal magnificence. In a spellbinding moment, her face changed into a mesmerizing kaleidoscope of a thousand beauties who took turns in manifesting and morphing from one face to the next, radiating all-encompassing splendor and love. Damian had never beheld such magic in his life and he stammered, "Are…are you the Earth Queen?" She nodded with a welcoming kiss on his forehead and said mysteriously, "And I am all women."

As if in a hypnotic trance, Damian let her glide him weightlessly through cascading liquid emeralds and floating crystal boulders, chambers upon chambers of sparkling gems and glittering diamonds that splashed rainbow prism in the atmosphere all around them. He instinctually knew he was in the center of the Earth. He looked at his self-assured companion in awe for confirmation with the question hanging on his lips. She validated his knowing with her eyes, as though reading his every thought. 'The center of the Earth is indeed a crystalline core!' Noted Damian with elation.

Days seemed to have gone by as Damian was submerged in the beatitude of his Queen's emanating love. Time and linear thoughts somehow evaporated. One morning they came upon a soft crystalline platform that felt luxuriously velvety when she bid him to make love to her, to which he responded with a relaxed naturalness that astounded his timid self. Not every day was a simple guy invited to partake the boudoir of the Earth Queen, yet he wasn't daunted. Her glorious body fanned out undulating layers of entrancing vitality that unfolded and enfolded as if she was the very dance of a jellyfish. He felt luscious feminine love enwrapping him; he joined in voraciously and with revering adoration. It was beyond any sexual encounters he ever had. The Queen did not exhibit any seductive pomposity, attitudes of game-playing or insecure provocations to test his prowess or taunt his inadequacies. Only joyous rapture was shared and his maleness was wholly welcome. Her radiant exquisiteness with a transcendent essence emanated a perfect purity of love. Damian felt his muscles and bulging nerves tightened, his erect maleness grew hard as it engorged with blood, his body burned with desire as he never had before. He eagerly seized her, pushing his way inside her bottomless well and plunging deeply into the unknown of her mystery. He discharged himself and unleashed the greatest torrents of love flow, erupting in unending waves of immeasurable love for her, as though he had always known her intimately. With a final thrust of unstoppable tides of pleasure, he thundered the roar of a lion, commanding the majesty of his forest kingdom.

They basked in a divine spirit of total abandon for each other, for the world, for all of life. The sexual osmosis with this celestial being had humbled Damian into a new awakening of veneration for the enigma of the feminine. Their union seemed to him to convey a healing of hearts intended for a purpose greater than himself, as though he carried the matrix of all men to be blessed by the sublime feminine without being judged on any of their shortcomings. Damian was enraptured beyond questioning why she chose him as her lover, as though their sexual intimacy was something he knew all his life. Her coming into his dream world during his childhood was the prelude to this glorious culmination. It was in truth what his heart had been searching for all these years, and he accepted her love with a complete acceptance of himself.

Life, however, was not so mercifully idyllic to make it possible for him to slip away from the mundane. One day, Damian heard sounds of chirping birds emerging through the woods, and gurgling brooks beckoning him back to the dimensions of this world. Insects were buzzing about as he brushed the dry leaves off his rumpled clothes, when he rose suddenly from the hard ground and heard echoes of cars whirring by from the distant highway. He panicked for a moment; he didn't know how many days had elapsed since his fall into the netherworld. He didn't have any recollection about how he had been brought back to the woods where he had begun his journey. He searched for the cell phone that was still in his pocket; he looked at the time and date— it was Monday at 11 am. The number 11 was always a magical number to him. It seemed to open doorways for him to the unconscious! Damian was incredulous. He felt as if he had spent days with his beloved Queen, but it was actually less than twenty-four hours since his plunge into the abyss of Eden. Damian wished he had the luxury of time to think through this incoherence, but his pragmatic mind urged him to gather his wits and go back to work right away. He avoided checking whether he had any cell phone messages. His instinct told him he was late for something, very late.

When Damian rushed into his workplace, Richard, the engineer, gushed out anxiously, "Where the hell were you? We kept calling and you didn't answer your phone! Do you remember there was a meeting with Peter this morning? He was furious!" Damian's heart sank. He knew he really had screwed up badly this time. There had already been incidents in recent months between Peter and him. Peter's company had invested money that largely funded the R&D of his recent invention. Missing the important meeting this morning to go over the progress of his design was indefensible, as Peter had specifically flown into town for this reporting. Damian muttered some lame excuse to Richard and started dialing Peter's number, knowing he had no choice but face the consequences of his inexcusable and apparent negligence. The mundane world was harsh, but he had to tend to it.

What an irony. Just moments ago, he had been utterly altered by the most earth-shattering experience of his entire existence, yet he had no one to confide in or celebrate with, at least not now. Even his closest friends would question his sanity at such a bizarre tale.

He couldn't bear any ridicule for the time being, even if he was burning to tell someone, anyone.

Damian spent the ensuing months working fourteen-hour days, refining the designs and testing them late into the night to make it up to Peter and his colleagues. He was secretly amazed how new ideas sparked inside of him and how technical challenges were solved miraculously one by one. He had now stumbled into a new meditative state of working. He couldn't sleep most nights with his mind racing about his day job problems and his body inflamed with yearning to be with his Queen again. She came to him now and then in hazy form, not quite visible in 3-D reality, and yet so tangible to him. He knew that she wasn't only a figment of his imagination. Their lovemaking was intoxicating beyond any worldly pleasures that he ever had. Their intercourse was palpable, which was so different than self-indulged masturbation.

Curiously, it was always after their union that she taught him in his dream state how to solve his design gridlock, such as weaving the straw cables in tight and impeccable braids. He and his Queen had become the entwined tresses when she taught him how to sensually dance with abandon. They were the core of the shamanic trance of a kundalini dance that interlaced the fibers, which his engineering mind could not have ever figured out on its own. She teased him and semi-solemnly told him that the invention of his technology was her instigation to begin with. Its significance was to help her solve many of the environmental problems that plagued her well-being. The more farm by-products that were used beneficially without needing to burn them, the less carbon dioxide would overwhelm the stratosphere and aggravate global warming. Damian and his crew already knew the impact this invention would have on the carbon footprints in large-scale construction projects worldwide. How could the Earth Queen not be his Muse? Together, she was his most natural partner to work on this life-sustaining creation.

What amazed him was how technically adept her mind was. She would challenge and debate with him engineering details that even Richard had not brought up. During these developments, his ego would be tested time and again; he realized how limited his linear thinking often was in comparison to the all-pervasive infinite mind of the divine feminine. She guided him with love to sink into his whole being and to allow all that arose from his inner knowing. He was continually being elevated and clarified in his state of awakening through the stages of the technical progresses.

"You have cultivated yourself for lifetimes to embody the fullness of your soul; you are close to achieving it at this point in your existence. From now on, don't bring old fears and concerns about responding to life as you had in the past. Do not carry expectations of disappointing yourself in anything that you do. Your unique energetic signature is the spark from which infinite resources flow from you," she said firmly yet with so much love. With these words, she encouraged him at each turn not to give in to his frustration or self-doubt. Their precious time together alternated between loving resplendently and refining his technical designs, while Damian was inebriated in the pool of their shared essence. There was nothing he'd rather do than be in ecstasy with her and to serve her greater purpose. This was what he defined as his *Great Work*.

Sometimes Damian was at a loss, though, how to assess the recent phenomenon, let alone how to relate to his friends the Queen's delicious nocturnal visits. There were hardly any references he could consult with or get any support from on what was happening in his life. At times he was afraid that he might have encountered a succubus who had latched onto him, but none of the manifestations of her amorous ways had any hint of darkness or demonic twists to it. He wasn't afraid nor was he tormented psychically. If anything, the Spirit Queen had enhanced his life by leaps and bounds. He felt empowered beyond any limits and he was energized to no ends.

His mind was focused, his intuition clear, and he found himself needing less and less sleep. His shamanic gifts were greatly augmented. Damian inadvertently was blessed with a new way of helping people to cope better with their life problems, whether of a neurotic, depressive or psychotic nature. He discovered that during meditation his spirit body could enter into people's *House of Being*—a place where the soul dwells—to observe how people were at the mercy of their subconscious minds, no matter how diligently they had worked on themselves psychologically or spiritually to overcome nagging shadows and pains. In the *House of Being*, Damian would negotiate with the dark entities that were inevitably there, whether they were an intrinsic part of the person's soul or parasitical spirits who freeloaded on the energy of the person in question. His assistance was so effective that more and more people sought his help. He had now become an inventor by day and a shaman by night, with hardly any time to sleep; yet he was full of energy still.

He poured through all the books he could get his hands on that dealt with the theme of men's relationships with phantoms and underworld queens. The closest reference he came upon was the famous story of Thomas the Rhymer—the 13th century Scottish laird and reputed prophet who had gained supernatural power, which rivaled that of Merlin. Thomas was alleged to have spent several years serving as lover to the Queen of Elfland in the underworld before emerging back into the world with prophetic supremacy and 'a tongue that could not lie'.

However, Damian noticed that his relationship with the Earth Queen didn't parallel the old tales of the knights in service to their queens who dominated them. The experience of their intimacy had forged a new path of love that merged the masculine and the feminine in a co-creative partnership, with the multidimensional manifested into the three-dimensional. She became fused with him in his daily life, and he didn't have to disappear again in the chasm. It was this very synthesis into oneness that had welded so naturally in the awakening of his inexhaustible inner world. She had amply revealed to him that Earth was indeed a sentient consciousness who felt all the feelings of humans in magnified proportions and who possessed extraordinary senses beyond the comprehension of current consensus.

Her voice of despair on the abuses inflicted upon her, her voice of compassion and hope for change, her voice of strength and clarity inspired him to finish his invention. The end product of his development would be an affordable building material of immense flexibility, adaptable in using residual cultivations of harvests anywhere in the world. The effect on saving resources and using renewable crops would be enormous. By using local farm wastes, long distance transportations to bring products to the building sites would be reduced, not to mention minimizing deforestation and many other environmental benefits. Besides, the low impact, low cost, non-toxic, hand-fed method of manufacturing, utilizing unskilled labor anywhere, would be revolutionary for the construction business. However, Damian was not naïve about the built-in resistance of the giant corporations in the industry. That would be another great hurdle to cross when the time came.

Five months later, a working prototype was

completed. This acceleration of technical success impressed even Peter who was generally hard to please. Damian couldn't tell anyone that it wasn't his brilliant mind that achieved the results; that it was the Earth Queen herself who had taken over the reign. A sample batch of the product and the machine were shipped to the most prominent national testing center for approval and certification. Damian privately dreaded the ensuing bureaucracy—which would be unavoidable, especially with the extreme restrictions of the current building codes, not to mention the powerful resistance of the would-be-threatened giant corporations dominating the building industry. Damian could but think and work one step at a time. During this interval, Damian had a respite he so badly needed. He took a week off and flew to the Yucatan. He loved diving through the caverns of the cenotes—the pristine fresh water sinkholes unique to this region—to swim away the demands of his daily life.

One morning as Damian followed a trail winding its way through lush green valleys, he came upon an unspoiled cenote off the beaten track. He was thrilled that no one was around, and since he didn't have his diving gear with him, he just stripped and plunged into the crystal clear water. He completely let go and relaxed into being lulled in this womb-like cradle, feeling waves of profound calm. Suddenly he had a faint awareness of being swirled into a sensuous vortex of energy. He nonchalantly opened his eyes and was shocked to have the Earth Queen snuggled naked in his embrace. It dawned on him in that moment that water was her main domain. Why hadn't it occurred to him that he might meet her while immersed in it? He excitedly wanted to kiss her, but instead, they were together catapulted into a funnel of deep warmth. Damian felt the molecules of his entire being dissolve into the void of infinity—the liberation from the confinement of his 3-D form was an exhilaration he'd never experienced before. It was as though he had dropped into the omniscient mind of God, observing all that was happening to him. In this surreal weightlessness and formlessness, they arrived in a crystalline water temple beyond any earthly architecture he had ever seen. There were shimmering translucent spirit beings all around the glittering columns of quartz and aquamarine to welcome them in joyous anticipation. Damian had a sense of déjà vu poised on the edge of remembrance of the boundlessness of his soul. He had somehow known this place for eternities.

In an aura of penetrating radiance through wave-like transmissions, his Queen beckoned him to prepare for a shamanic initiation of sexual rite. Damian relished the invitation with total surrender and trust in her. Neither of them or anything else around them was in solid form. It was as though they were just bubbles of luminosity communicating with each other, yet he still saw and felt everything. Penetrating the unfathomable depth of his body-less Queen in sexual communion had raised his Eros to devotional heights of piety. He felt her energy transposed onto his and he became her emotions. His familiar senses and male erection were no longer existent; he had become *her* and her ecstasy. At first, a silky languor spread throughout his body, he slipped into abandon and wanton delight for welcoming, for wanting to be filled up. Then a surge of titillating sensations swept over his thighs. He felt more tremulous, his nipples erect with heightened sensations, yet he didn't have a body! He had become a fluid channel from which her pleasure flowed. The world around him turned into a whirling pool of light where he was no more. Damian cried out waves and shockwaves of climatic cascades, one topping the other, continuously. For the first time in his life, he thoroughly experienced the full potency of woman in her endless shudders of pleasure. Damian sighed with an immense satisfaction: 'if men only knew the power of a woman's orgasm in all her glorious mystery!'

Being submerged in such an immeasurable depth of the very womb of Earth and simultaneously being her, an all-encompassing feminine eminence came alive within him. Damian's masculine ego consciousness attained a transcendental illumination. The shamanic dream, love and sex had now melded into an awareness of an inner feminine that was all-woman but more-than-human. Earth's sexual heights in him brought him to a total luminescence rather than a limited male consciousness of having just fragmented knowledge of the feminine.

Beholding her sumptuous response inside his masculine potency was a phenomenon of planetary magnificence meeting divine brilliance through human awareness. Her amalgamation into him became a mind-altering and transformative psychic force, an assimilation of male-female fullness within himself. Damian understood in that moment of bliss why men, since time immemorial, had the insatiable obsession to possess women and land. It was the primal yearning to come home to the oneness with *All There Is*. No material possessions could ever quench their thirst or stop their furious acts of greed in plundering and ravaging resources until they came to prostrate before the *All Feminine* as he did that day. Somehow the wisdom of Tao slipped into his consciousness and he understood the depth of its meaning for the first time in his life—the timeless ancient philosophy of the Chinese that had aligned with nature all along, of which the cerebral West forever struggled to fathom.

> The Tao that can be told is not the eternal Tao…
> The nameless is the beginning of Heaven and Earth,
> The named is the Mother of all things.
> Ever desireless, one can see the mystery,
> Ever desiring, one beholds the manifestations.
> These two spring from the same source but differ in name;
> This is the Void of creation.
> Void within the Void,
> The gate to all mystery.

Earth—home to all living forms, was the *nameless* consciousness manifested into a *named* three-dimensional planet. She had been re-inventing herself for eons with geological shifts and shocks, and compassionately absorbing the strife of human idiocies and the wonder of human evolution. Until all men became lovers of her welcoming embrace, the unending abuses in all of their permutations would perpetuate. A sudden clarity enlightened Damian's mind: he was not her only chosen lover. She had been whispering through the millennia to all who would hear her heartsongs. Thousands of naturalists through the ages had defended and preserved virgin lands for generations to enjoy; many devoted environmentalists had been tirelessly educating the masses to save the polluted oceans. Indeed, in just the last hundred years, there have been indefatigable efforts to bring the new conscious evolution about no matter how disconsolate the global situations were on the surface.

How Earth Spirit had chosen him to express herself sexually was another display of her astonishing sentience. He was one of her beloved who had been listening to her heartbeat his whole life. He was certain that everyone who felt and loved Earth was assigned a particular calling to help usher in the New Earth with his or her innate gifts and passion. Damian's task was to share with the world her potent aliveness, in whatever way he could help to bring about the awakening of sacred sexuality, between humans, between all sentient beings, and ultimately between all forms of consciousness. Earth was the macro cognizance who has been concerting and guiding the evolution of consciousness all along, with the loving help of a multitude of otherworldly beings, followed by humans who listened to the unfolding of the greater whole.

'Doesn't every life form on Earth spring from sexual union? Why wouldn't the Earth herself feel sexually alive? Why would humans be so arrogant as to think that our planet is only landmasses and oceans to take from with such complacency?' It was with these reflections that Damian emerged from the cenote. He had lost track of time. He found his pile of clothes and his watch; it was only five in the afternoon. He was once again stunned how he was reeled into a timelessness that had stretched beyond space, beyond boundless horizons.

Damian aimlessly drove into a nearby small village looking for food, realizing he was famished. The town looked forsaken and rather dilapidated, like many other little Mayan villages dotting along the Yucatan, in sharp contrast to the garish high rises of beach-cities that were drowned with tourists. There were no restaurants or cafés in sight. He spotted a young woman making tortillas under a hut. He parked and walked toward the delightful smell coming out of the fire pit. He was so hungry he was happy to eat just plain tortillas. A couple of people bought from the vendor and chattered with her about what appeared to him familiar pleasantries. Damian handed her a rather large bill of peso and pointed to the tortillas. She indicated she didn't have enough change for it. Damian rummaged in his pockets but he didn't find any change. She giggled and handed him a big stack of tortillas on a square piece of banana leaf that served as a plate, and gestured to him that he could have them for free. He was deeply touched by her spontaneous generosity. He knew how poor these people were and how every peso counted, yet this gentle soul willingly offered free food to a gringo! He thanked her profusely with broken Spanish, and she handed him a bottle of water with a big smile. He was choked up by such kind-heartedness. He always felt at home with indigenous people, no matter what country they were from or what tribal customs they had. He felt connected to them through a heart language that the self-proclaimed civilized world didn't deem important.

An elderly man appeared out of nowhere as Damian was wolfing down the delicious stove-hot tortillas. The man introduced himself as Chac. He surprisingly spoke very good English. When he saw the astonished delight on Damian's face, he explained that he had a past career in tourism where he dealt with lots of foreigners. His eyes and square-jawed face revealed a deep wisdom, and Damian was so happy he could communicate with someone in this desolate town. He told Chac that he had come from swimming in the nearby cenote, though there was no point in disclosing the enormity of his encounter with the Earth Goddess. Chac thoughtfully commented that the cenotes were sacred to his people. He went on to say they were mystical chambers that synchronized the heartbeat of Earth to the frequencies of Heaven, which powerful vibrations flowed naturally in the human hearts. Anyone with sensitivity and who paid attention to the exceptional vortex energy while submerged in a cenote will remember their oneness with the mystery of the Universe. Then Chac rather enigmatically conveyed in a whispering tone, "In these sacred wells, only shamans find the passageways to the underworld for initiation." He winked at Damian as if he knew what had happened to him. Chac asked whether

Damian would go for a walk with him. Damian happily obliged, but before they sauntered off, he felt the urge to hand a 50-peso bill to the young woman behind the steamy tortillas. She refused but Damian insisted, asking Chac to translate for him his gratefulness for her big heart. Her eyes filled up with tears.

They walked down a path shadowed by huge palm trees. Damian's engineering mind stopped him in his tracks to check out the strength of the palm frond. He had known all along that it was one of the strongest materials he could use for his invention, but to see its abundance and feel it in person just thrilled him with inspiration. As he was cutting through a stalk with his Swiss-Army knife and examining it, Chac commented on the decrepitude of his haphazard town. He remarked how the locals had good skills to weave beautiful thatch roofs with palm fronds that could last for years, but they had no architectural or industrial concepts about how to make their ramshackle village into a unified whole. They sorely needed planning help, but the government hardly paid any attention to their requests.

It broke Damian's heart to witness the continuous suffering of the Mayan people since the Spanish eradicated their ancient splendors in the 1500s. He inquired about Chac's role in this town. It turned out that he was the Shaman Elder who served as Medicine Man-Town Planner-Enterprise Council for the community. Damian expressed an interest to help give him some technical guidance on construction and planning, stating that he had built many housing projects before. A big smile of gratitude spread over Chac's wrinkled face. He invited Damian to spend a few days with him in his humble shack so he could show him the layout of the town and introduce people to him. Damian spontaneously accepted. The next few days were some of the richest of his life.

They spent long hours talking into the night, under starry skies, about esoteric wisdom and the Mayan Calendar. Even the mosquitoes and annoying insects buzzing about didn't bother him anymore; he was so engrossed in sharing shamanic views with Chac. Damian asked for his opinion of the Mayan Prophecy about 2012, and Chac observed in a most unassuming way: "The West has stirred such a fuss over the end of time, making up so many fearful stories about the end of the world. What our ancestors meant was the end of time, as we know it today. As three-dimensional ways of living gradually dissolve, more and more people will be experiencing life as dream-walking into the multi-dimensional, where normal and paranormal will blend onto one. Science will no longer be able to hold their logical supremacy. Mystical events that they cannot explain will seep into many people's lives; gradually people will accept these events as natural after a while. Those who cannot accept living the new way will subconsciously choose to leave this world. There will also be massive earth changes for Mother Earth to rebalance herself. She will be speaking directly into people's hearts how she is guiding all of us to the next evolution, merging our consciousness with hers and with our cosmic brothers and sisters." Chac made a grand gesture of embracing the twinkling lights in the sky. At that point, Damian felt so relieved to hear such a straightforward knowing of the Prophecy. Chac had described in plain terms what had been happening in Damian's life; the multi-dimensional occurrences that had turned his 3-D life upside down.

In a gush of eagerness and a yearning to confide to someone who might understand, he told Chac of how the Earth Queen had drastically changed his life in recent months and how she had led him to complete his invention. He also told of his encounter in the cenote, albeit awkwardly. He felt utterly relieved that he could share the most sacred experience of his life with this wise man, with whom Damian felt a keen bonding. The bizarre story didn't faze Chac, instead his eyes were filled with tears of appreciation and he exclaimed: "Only a true shaman will die the death of his ego, when he ultimately becomes the full male-female within himself, in his body and in his spirit. Until a man breathes the mighty life force of woman, he cannot fully embrace himself and the world without conquering and dominance." Chac then told of a premonition given to him by Mother Earth a year ago during a summer solstice meditation, that one day a white man would come along with gifts of technology to help rebuild their village, and that this know-how was her creation to solve many problems for the ecosystem. She also told him that their joining of hands would not only be a symbolic act of redemption for the white men who had decimated his people, but it would also be one of the events to help shift the separation of humanity into a flourishing era of oneness, linking human hearts around the globe by a new invisible thread, manifesting a piece of the Mayan Prophecy of man's co-creation with Earth. Chac added that she described this white man as a pure-hearted soul who had devoted himself for lifetimes to planetary evolutions.

Damian was all at once awed and humbled that such a revelation might have anything to do with him. He would so gladly give of his time and his technology to assist these people, but he also wondered how he would come up with the funding to make it a reality. His company was surviving on a shoestring, and Peter was already threatening not to invest any more money into the next phase of developments. Nonetheless, he knew too that destiny work was not up to his control; things would unfold in alignment with the greater forces. The serendipity of meeting Chac right after his cenote's encounter didn't escape him. He also noted the cosmic humor on the name Chac in relation to his invention— its symbolic meaning being the God of Agriculture who bestowed rain to the world and gave it abundance.

Chac took Damian around town and introduced him to makeshift technicians and handymen who were active in rebuilding the village. Their welcoming innocent joy was heartwarming and invigorating. They were all eager and willing to work for the good of the community and they listened with enthusiasm to Damian's suggestions. Damian also found out that there were hardly any strict building codes in these indigenous villages, which would be a natural place to try out his technology. There was so much support and ready help besides the bountiful palm frond and other organic materials to build with. In the midst of these excitements, he got a most auspicious email from his office manager when he went to the only Internet café in a nearby town. A grant among several other grants that he had applied for long ago in anticipation of a pilot project, which he almost had forgotten about, had just been approved. It was a modest award of $35,000 that he couldn't do much with if he were to conduct the project in the States, but it was enough to make a lot happen here. He was overwhelmed by the magic of the moment.

Damian was ecstatic, and he jubilantly shared this timely good news with Chac who instantly dropped to his knees and kissed the ground. They both knew this synchronicity was another magical manifestation of the greater forces at work. Damian knew realistically of the challenges ahead of him with Peter who most likely would fight tooth and nail against bringing the pilot to a blip of a poor village in the Yucatan, but then none of this was really up to him. Destiny had swooshed him up from that day in the forest where he had met the Earth Queen and it had since propelled him on a path of no return. A path that he would surrender to and protect for the rest of his life. Damian's heart opened wide with confidence and immense joy.

Afterword

"I am transmuting from tired, abused and undeserving
Into fully remembering
My devotion to the magnificence in the making."

 Afterword

WHILE I WAS ABOUT to publish this book in 2012, Earth-Spirit surprised me in a dream and guided me to place the poem, *Earth's Revelations,* as the climax for this book. When I had "scribed" her yearnings in 2010, she expressly conveyed to me not to doubt her transmission, and not to edit 'her words'. I verbally delivered the poem to an audience in Ashland, Oregon on July 18, 2010, during the weekend of worldwide events for the Conscious Convergence—based on two important dates of the Mayan Calendar that propelled forward humanity's evolutionary consciousness.

The poem itself contains profound messages that are beyond the scope of this book, therefore my puzzlement about including it, yet Earth has always been accurate on her precise directions. All living beings on this Earth are bound to this World Soul in more magical ways than ever fathomed; we are now just slowly awakening to the meaning of Deep Ecology. The love stories in this book—be it between humans or with spirit beings—are but microcosm of her magnificent matrix.

Human imaginations have brought forth civilizations, material and technological sophistications, yet we are more and more alienated from one another.

With wars and the pillaging of our beloved Earth unabated, humanity's malaise and suffering continue. I invite you to extend your imaginations beyond contemporary science, religions or empirical researches, to take a leap of faith and hear the voice of our World Soul. Her sentience is not just an esoteric concept or a poetic notion—she is the essence that permeates through every living entity in our realm. Her guiding wisdom comes into an even more poignant focus in current times.

May Earth's poem, on the pages that follow, inspire you to listen to her breath in your heart.

Earth's Revelations

A Tribute to the Conscious Convergence on July 18, 2010

I HAVE, from the spark of life immemorial,

Abided by a codified destiny

As the Planet of Choice

For individuation.

In evolution and involution through the billion years,

I've fashioned myself into the Three-Dimensional

As a platform for the divine annals

To hold resonance

For a human race,

Made of starseeded love,

For a Grand Experiment.

Born forgetting, you have labored through

Strenuous tests of duality

To ultimately return to unity

By choice, back into remembrance.

LOVE, the amrita of life effervescence,

Emanating from the crystalline core of me,

Has always been fused with light

Of the Sun's luminescence.

He is my beloved, my consort—your life progenitor.

My unconditional love nurtures his brilliance;

Our seed in each other completes the human circuitry,

Matrix of Heaven on Earth's conscious destiny.

Feminine strength—fused with my quantum patterns,
When broken through illusions of subservience or manipulation,
You become vessels of love, forgiveness and compassion.
Masculine strength—fused with the Sun's radiance,
When shedding skins of the serving knights, controllers or dominators,
You remember your rightful place as life giving protectors and lovers.
Creative alchemy of the Sun in Male
Activates the ambrosia of Earth in Female.

Feel my heartbeat inside of your heartbeat,
I am you with magnified emotions, pulsating and reverberating
Your feelings in ten thousand folds.
When you hurt, I deluge in flooding
And erupt in molten lava unleashing.
When you rejoice in ecstatic harmony,
I blossom in a thousand petals,
Sing with the breaching whales,
And soar with the majestic eagles.
Yin and Yang in exquisite balance,
Not in opposing frictions.

When my Sentience comes alive from within you,
My Sovereignty becomes you.
When you make my civil rights your civil rights,
Abuse and squandering of me will dissolve away.
Men become my lovers,
Women my manifestors.

Then and naturally then,

I will be speaking through tens of thousands of you,

No matter your race, creed or vocation.

All of you are aspects of me and of the Sun,

Joyful in Oneness with all living beings,

To return to the fold of our original intention.

THERE ARE no outside forces to victimize you,

No greed out there can be sustained

Without your participation.

No power or political oppressions can intimidate you

Without your acquiescence, fear or indolent compliance.

You look skyward for ascension

While your Merkaba is right at your feet.

I am your source to the multiverse and your anchor,

I am your macro splendor.

I weave the cosmic alchemy,

You decode the mystery of omniscience.

Rise above misguided beliefs

That render my crystalline core as dark and hellish.

Is it any wonder your hearts are muffled and full of anguish?!

I AM TRANSMUTING from tired, abused and undeserving

Into fully remembering

My devotion to the magnificence in the making.

You are not saving me for your own ends,

To satisfy your survival and your illusive plans.

It is me leading you out of your quandary
Onto your next evolutionary destiny.
I beckon you to transcend dominance or victimhood
To co-create with me our Celestial Onehood.
Dissolve your egocentric contemplations
Into responsible actions of compassion.

HONOR ME as Lady Earth,
Do no longer rely on me as Mother Earth.
Yes, I am your mother lode of consciousness
But not your co-dependent fear manifest.
Reflect on your habits, your indulgence and your deeds,
Free yourselves from your insatiable needs.
Your hearts are wise with infinite capacity
To live as rings of love fused with light and dignity.

I WILL be guiding you
To ride waves of parallel realities;
It is your choice to manifest the Prophecy.
In union with Self and Source
We end the illusion of separation.
We, together in Conscious Partnership,
Co-align our destinies
With converging unity
Back to our Divine Sovereignty.

About the Artists

GAELYN LARRICK (Book Cover Artist)
An award-winning book designer who has been crafting book covers for many authors, Gaelyn is also a mixed media artist whose passion is to create glimpses of humanity's connection to something intuitively known but not always obvious. Her creative process allows her to step outside of time and into a place of flow where she finds herself in a dance of discovery with colors and textures. Through images and words, she conjures up an idealistic and usually surrealistic view of the world that invites people to unite with their own divine nature. Gaelyn lives in Talent, Oregon with her husband Bram.

TORY ELENA (Book Illustration Artist)
"Artist: [noun] A prime specimen of the deconstructed construction of the continuously implosive explosion."
—*Tory Elena*

Tory Elena is an artist whose work is a snapshot of visions from her dreams of night and day. As an illustrator, painter, sculptor, prop maker, installation artist, and storyboard artist—art expands beyond a career to her very way of life. Bridging the worlds of sight and sound, Tory Elena explores synesthesia as both composer and drummer in the band Sea At Last. She is also a board member of GYPSYPOP RECORDS.

XIONG SHENG (Contributing Artist)

Xiong Sheng is a direct descendent of the Naxi people—one of the primordial indigenous tribes of China, which spans over 6000 years, who live near the beautiful city of LiJiang, China. He and his family owned a small sculpture gallery in Lijiang. His art stays true to the form, wisdom and knowledge of the ancient legends of his people, while his style has been modernized for the sensitivity of contemporary aesthetics.

Note: Starseeds Reunited, *on page 86, is a replicated likeness of a wood sculpture made by Xiong Sheng that Jacqueline Sa bought in Lijiang in 2005 at his art gallery. In order to stay true to the original Naxi art for the tale's veracity, Jacqueline requested Tory Elena to create a pen-and-ink drawing similar to the sculpture. Since Jacqueline has been unable to communicate with Xiong Sheng, and has no knowledge whether his sculpture gallery still exists today, she herewith expresses her gratitude and respect for his beautiful art.*

www.rootslegends.com